THE
GOBBLIN'
SOCIETY

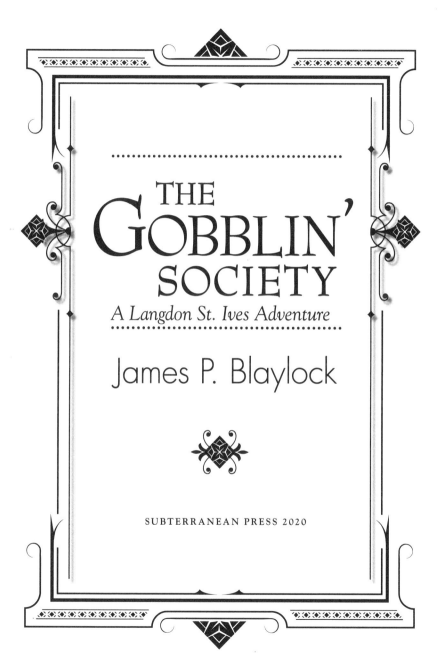

THE GOBBLIN' SOCIETY

A Langdon St. Ives Adventure

James P. Blaylock

SUBTERRANEAN PRESS 2020

First Edition

ISBN
978-1-59606-948-0

Subterranean Press
PO Box 190106
Burton, MI 48519

subterraneanpress.com

Manufactured in the United States of America

For Viki

CHAPTER One

A QUIET SUPPER

The half-timbered manor house, built in the Gothic style, stood on a prominence above the village of Broadstairs, well back from the sea. High and narrow, with bay windows and sharply peaked gables, it had been built some years before Broadstairs itself grew up along the chalk cliffs of the Kentish coast. A widow's walk on the southeast corner was partly obscured by the grove of elms and beeches that had risen around the manor over the last century.

From the eminence of the widow's walk, there was a view of the ships anchored in the Downs or steaming up from the Channel, and one could just make out the forward edge of Kingsgate Castle through the trees. On particularly clear nights moonlight shone on the Goodwin Sands, and in the pre-dawn darkness, a sharp eye might pick out smugglers running in toward convenient bays in swift-sailing luggers. There were arched shutters over the second story windows of the house, closed at night, which gave it a secretive air,

and when the house and high trees were veiled by a sea mist the old, grey manor simply vanished. Holiday travelers staying in one of the seaside hotels in Broadstairs might remain a month in the village and be unaware of the manor's existence. Local residents shunned it.

Julian Hobbes studied the house uneasily, having passed through the open gates and walked halfway along the long carriage drive that led up from the road. The shutters on the second floor windows were thrown open and he could make out a figure moving beyond the leafy shadows on the panes of glass. The sun was low in the sky, and it was later in the day than he would have chosen to arrive, given the spectral house that loomed above him. His coach had lost a wheel, however, coming out from Canterbury, and had taken hellfire long to repair.

He had no idea what welcome he would receive here, if any sort of welcome at all, but he was fairly certain that his mission did not warrant bringing a constable along. If there was trouble, the weighted stick that he carried would have to suffice. There was something off about the old house, something unsettling that he couldn't quite name. But it was a fanciful thought, and not being a fanciful man he dismissed it from his mind, knocked the head of his stick against his palm, and set out through the trees, determined to be comfortably aboard the evening coach that left for Canterbury in two hours.

IN THE WOOD-PANELED second-story room of the manor, three men sat at a heavily built dining table illuminated by

a candlelit chandelier. They were members of an eating club, the Gobblin' Society, and the old house in which they met was known by the whimsical members as Gobblin' Manor. Morbid anatomical paintings by the French artist Gericault hung on the wall. The table rested upon a central column cut from a section of hollowed-out tree trunk, which housed the mechanical workings that elevated food from the kitchen on the floor below. A silver platter had just come ratcheting up, covered in a high dome, and the bottle of claret had gone around for the second time, the four men getting by without the help of servants. Beside the domed platter lay a wooden board on which sat a loaf of dark bread and a long knife.

"I have it on good authority that my great grandfather dined on the corpse of the poet Chatterton," Harry Larsen said in a loud voice after awakening from a doze. As well as having the inconsiderate habit of falling asleep after a second glass of wine, Larsen boasted far too often about his doubtful ancestors. His nonsense was countenanced because he was rich. He had an abnormally large, round head with hair like frizz, and his nose angled slightly upward, revealing yet more frizz.

"I don't believe it, Larsen," Jason Forbes told him. "Chatterton's flesh would have been poisoned by the arsenic he drank when he murdered himself. And starving poets have no meat on their bones in any event. I've been told that they rarely eat well unless heavily sauced, and even then they're a stringy lot, like eating an old rooster." Forbes wore a lavender cravat with an amber stickpin in the center of the knot. A bee looked out from within the amber. Beside Forbes's chair hung

a gold-braided rope with royal blue ribbon threaded through it, and he fiddled with the rope as he spoke.

"Chatterton was *alleged* to have consumed arsenic," Larsen said. "My grandfather had knowledge to the contrary."

"Was your grandfather a poet, then?" asked the third man, the current President, whom the members of the Society called Southerleigh, although it was not his actual name. "We're enlivened and influenced by what we consume, after all." Southerleigh was an abnormally tall and skeletal figure, unsmiling unless the smile was contrived, who spoke while looking into the ruby contents of his wine glass through the pince-nez clinging to his nose.

"Indeed," Larsen said. "He was a minor poet, but a good one. Johnson admired his work."

"*Dictionary* Johnson?" Forbes asked skeptically.

"The very man."

"Then your grandfather should have dined on Johnson," Forbes said. "Johnson's plump corpse would have been far more unctuous than Chatterton's, and sweetened by genius into the bargain. Chatterton's poetry was unreadable, the maunderings of a clever boy who hadn't anything of his own to say."

The door opened and a man in servant's livery looked in. He had the appearance of a human ape, his arms hanging to his knees and a prominent forehead and oversized jaw. "A Mr. Julian Hobbes has arrived and has asked for an audience, sir," he said to the President. "Shall I turn him away, or is he expected?"

"*Hobbes*, do you say? Show him in, Jensen, and seat him in the draped chair. We are indeed expecting him."

THE GOBBLIN' SOCIETY

"Shall I unfasten the collar from its compartment?"

"Yes, and of course stand by once the door is secured and the gentleman is seated."

Jensen bowed, walked across to a heavily carved wardrobe cabinet, and opened its door. Inside, locked to an eye-hook, hung a circular, yoke-like wooden collar with holes in its perimeter, each hole adjacent to a small, iron turn-buckle. He produced a key, opened the lock so that the collar might be removed, and then left the room again, noiselessly shutting the door behind him.

A long moment later, Jensen ushered Hobbes into the room and intoned his name.

"Welcome, sir," Southerleigh said cheerfully. Jensen draped Hobbes's coat from a hook by the door and rested his weighted cane in an elephant's foot umbrella stand. Jensen stepped to the specified chair, which was draped from seat to floor by a floral-painted curtain. He swiveled the chair to the left, making it possible for Hobbes to sit down, and then swiveled the now-occupied chair back again until it clanked into place.

"Good day to you gentlemen," Hobbes said, looking around skeptically. He caught sight of the morbid paintings on the wall now—severed limbs and heads, a dismembered skeleton—and could not prevent a look of distaste from passing across his face. Being an entirely rational man he had little patience for quirkiness or fancy, morbid or otherwise, nor was he impressed by it.

"My name is Southerleigh," the President said to him cheerfully, "and my two compatriots are Mr. Forbes and Mr. Larsen. The bottle stands by you, Larsen."

"Why, so it does," Larsen said, pouring wine into an empty glass. "You'll drink a bumper of this capital claret, Mr. Hobbes?" He pushed it across to Hobbes, who nodded his thanks and tasted it.

"Very gratifying," Hobbes said.

"Mr. Julian *Hobbes!*" Southerleigh said now, peering at him through his pince-nez, which made his eyes seem unnaturally close together. "I could almost believe you to be the son of Hobbes the chemist—Canterbury Hobbes?"

"Yes, sir, I am."

"Then we're doubly happy to make your acquaintance. I knew your mother, in fact, although it was many years ago, and in another country, as The Bard would have it. Do you also have a scientific bent, sir?"

Hobbes stared at him for a moment, not quite knowing what to do with the reference to his mother. He decided to ignore it, however, and said, "I dabble in electronic medicine. I studied in Paris."

"Capital. An interesting field with a soaring future, to my mind. The world is electrifying at a prodigious rate."

Hobbes nodded in acquiescence and said, "To get to the point, gentlemen, I've come about my mother's death-book. I have it on good authority that the book might reside within this house."

"*Do you?*" asked the President. "I'm puzzled by what you tell me. What do you mean by her *death-book?* Can either of you gentlemen enlighten me?" He looked quizzically at Forbes and Larsen.

"Alas, no," Forbes said. "Our friend Larsen has the blood of a poet in his veins, however, bookish blood, perhaps…"

Larsen shook his head. "He jests, Mr. Hobbes. I have no use for books unless they're ledgers."

"I wish I could speak with more authority," Hobbes told them, "but I'm led to believe that the book contains my poor mother's memories, wishes, and regrets. Not overlarge—a quarto, probably, but richly bound. Truth to tell, I've never seen it. My father kept it under lock and key. He believes that there is something of her…*spirit*…in it. Her soul, let us say, and if it is not returned to him he will certainly die unhappily. I'm aware that it sounds fabulous, but there you have it."

"It grieves me to hear this," Southerleigh said to him, "but surely you speak metaphorically. You mean a *diary?*—perhaps in your mother's own hand? A memoir?"

"Something more esoteric apparently," Hobbes told him. "But the exact nature of the book is immaterial. What is material is that it was delivered to this very house by a scurrilous servant who stole it from my father's desk along with a small lamp and a jeweled bottle of lamp oil, all of it contained in a wooden box with my mother's name upon it. The servant confessed to the crime after we found a startlingly large sum of money hidden in his room, and it was he who sent me to this very house. My sole purpose is to fetch the lot of it home and to return the money to whoever purchased the book and the lamp. It is my father's *dying* wish, gentleman, and so it is necessarily my wish also."

"It's thoughtful of you to have brought the ill-gotten money along with you, Mr. Hobbes, but the three of us are mere drones,

and we speak in earnest when we tell you that we have no knowledge of the book and the attendant curiosities. Did this servant know the name of the man who purchased it?

"He believed the man to be a baron of some variety."

"Of *course*," Southerleigh said. "The Baron! This is entirely in his line. If this book was stolen by your servant, I assure you that the Baron had no knowledge of the theft itself and that he will return the book at once, or as soon as he can fetch it. The Baron is an honorable man. Will you wait for him, sir? He will join us shortly. Surely you'll take a bite of something to eat in the meantime? We're an eating society, as whimsical as that might sound."

"I had hoped to return to Canterbury aboard the post coach this very evening. It's been a trying day."

"Then drink another glass of wine and take your ease. You won't have long to wait, I believe. We intend to sample an interesting...*pâté*, as the French have it. It is best eaten with bread."

"Do you know that in the East," Larsen told him, grinning strangely at him now, "they eat the brains of living monkeys? They trepan them, do you see, and at table they remove the silver cap that has replaced the disk of skull and dig out the flesh with a spoon. Brain matter has something of the consistency of figgy-dowdy."

Hobbes stared at him in disbelief. "Apparently you enjoy practicing on strangers, sir. But I won't be put off. I must insist that the book be returned to me. I'm prepared to pay for it in full, as I've said. I don't expect anyone to lose a farthing. I'll reiterate: it is the wish of my dying father, and I mean to see his wish granted. I am not at all in a mood for jesting."

The three men regarded him for a time without speaking. Hobbes glanced uneasily at the door, which was shut tight, and he saw that his walking stick no longer sat in the ridiculous elephant receptacle. The heavy shutters were closed over the windows now. He could not see the servant, but he sensed that the man stood behind him.

"Forgive me," he said, abruptly deciding to change his course. "My weariness has made me short tempered. I'm afraid my words were offensive to you."

"Not at all, Mr. Hobbes," the President said. "Our friend Larsen has an arcane sense of humor. We wouldn't conceive of eating a monkey unless it was thoroughly stewed, and we very much regret that your father is dying, although all of us must tread that dark road from which, the poets assure us, no man returns. You'll agree that some of us are condemned to tread upon it sooner than others." He smiled so broadly now that his cheeks pushed his eyes half shut and revealed uncannily sharp incisors. "Mr. Forbes," he said, "raise the dome and cut Mr. Hobbes a slice of cerebellum, if you will, ha ha!"

"Ho for a slice of cerebellum!" Forbes shouted, tipping back the hinged dome and making antic faces at Hobbes, apparently having suddenly lost his mind.

Hobbes saw to his horror that a man's severed head sat upon the platter. There was the smell of curry, evidently from the pool of yellowish-green sauce that was afloat with oyster mushrooms. Then Hobbes saw that he was mistaken: the head sat upon its own neck. The platter surrounding the neck fit like an Elizabethan ruff, but made of silver instead of lace. It was a

living head, the mouth mumbling soundlessly, the victim's body concealed beneath the draped table.

Hobbes attempted to push himself to his feet, but the servant took him by the shoulders and slammed him down into his chair. Forbes reached up and gave the dangling golden braid a tremendous yank. Hobbes heard a clatter of meshing gears and felt a heavy vibration from beneath him. Suddenly he was unable to move at all, his hands pinned to his sides, and he realized in a wave of horror that a wooden keg had risen from the floor and encircled his chair with him in it, the chair's drape having been drawn upward, spilling out around his kegged shoulders now like a winding sheet. He made another desperate attempt to push himself up using his legs alone, pitching his upper body backward to shake off the servant, but his knees were too tightly contained by the keg, and the chair was immovable.

The servant stepped away now, and a bare moment later a heavy wooden collar descended over Hobbes's head and rested atop the keg, covering his shoulders. Turnbuckles snapped-to, imprisoning him in his upright coffin, and with that he had become a natural companion to the man whose monstrous head still gibbered on the platter, the tongue lolling as if endeavoring to slurp up the curry sauce.

"Our friend will go out with the current lot, I believe," Southerleigh said to Larsen and Forbes with no hint of humor now. "And with haste—before any of his meddlesome friends come looking for him. Eat up, gentlemen. We have work to do when the Baron arrives."

Forbes lifted the silver disk that had neatly covered the top of the man's shaven pate, thereby exposing the convolutions of the brain. The man himself had fainted dead away now, out of fear or perhaps pain. The only evidence of life was the movement of his eyes behind the eyelids.

Southerleigh, nodding his satisfaction, unrolled a damask napkin from which tumbled an array of pickle forks and honed spoons.

CHAPTER Two

THE INHERITANCE

A lice St. Ives sat in a pleasantly amazed stupor, only half listening to Mr. Bayhew, the St. Ives's solicitor, who had come down from London to Aylesford to explain the details of Alice's sudden inheritance—a house on the coast some distance below Margate that had belonged to her Uncle Godfrey Walton. *Seaward*, it was named—a word that brought forth strange but mostly pleasant memories when Alice recalled it or heard it uttered. It was a practical name as well: perched midway down a cliff, the lonely house looked out across the Strait of Dover. The inheritance had been bound up in legal complications for so many years that the thought of it had diminished in her mind, fading from something wonderfully hypothetical to something merely lost. Now it was suddenly found.

It was her second inheritance. Several years back she and her husband Langdon had moved from Chingford into their present house in Aylesford Village, which had been

left to her by her Aunt Agatha Walton, Godfrey Walton's sister. Alice had no need of a *second* house, which seemed extravagant to a fault, she being a woman and with only a remote claim on either of the houses.

The family, including young Finn Conrad, who had found them several years ago and stayed on as an honorary member of the family, sat around the dinner table. They had eaten the better part of a twenty-pound sucking pig stuffed with sage and onions, along with roast potatoes and a vast salad made of lettuces and herbs grown in the garden, tossed with a dressing of mashed boiled eggs, French olive oil, and Stilton cheese.

Tubby Frobisher and his Uncle Gilbert, both of them round men weighing some eighteen stone, had eaten their share. They were staying downriver in the village of Snodland, Gilbert having recently assumed proprietorship of the Majestic Paper Mill. They had arrived at the St. Ives's house this afternoon bearing a machine for turning out frozen custard in stupefying quantities and also a vast basket of early-summer blueberries with which to flavor the custard.

A bottle of port stood in the center of the table now, along with biscuits, but was largely ignored in favor of coffee served out in mugs, the beans shipped in from Sumatra to Gilbert's mansion in Dicker, roasted and ground not a half hour past. Gilbert was as rich as Croesus, although generous to a fault and often given to rash behavior. His nephew Tubby looked very like Gilbert's twin, but with more hair on his head and thirty years younger.

Eddie and Cleo, the St. Ives children, were included despite the late hour, both of them amazed and happy, although Alice

noted that Cleo's eyes were half closed. Hodge the cat had sneaked onto Cleo's lap and fallen asleep, which even Hodge knew wasn't allowed at the table. Household rules had gone by the board. Alice watched Langdon's face as he listened keenly to what Bayhew had to say, but after a moment or two of paying attention, her thoughts drifted into the past.

Her late uncle's property, *her* property now, was an eccentric, rambling, isolated house a half a mile below the North Foreland Light. It stood above a deserted beach, where, in her childhood, Alice had spent countless weeks in the summer months, rambling along the seaside in complete and glorious freedom, looking into tidal pools and sea caves, and scavenging treasures thrown up onto the beach along that notoriously deadly stretch of coastline.

Her summer visits to *Seaward* had been shared with her cousin Collier, who had been a cheerful youth, gangly and often silly-minded and likely to be in trouble with their uncle for looking into locked rooms when he'd been told not to. The cousins had gone out rowing in the dory on calm days, sometimes as far out as the Goodwin Sands, and had trudged through the woods behind the house and fished for trout in the chalk streams. They had earned their room and board by cooking breakfasts and late suppers, most often leaving their uncle's food on a plate in the kitchen and clearing up the remains the following day. Alice's visits to *Seaward* had ended abruptly when she was thirteen years old.

Cousin Collier had simply disappeared out of her life at that same time, their respective families having no contact. Some six years later Collier had allegedly hanged himself after being disinherited by their uncle, who had no children of his own.

That had been another source of guilt, since Alice had *not* been disinherited. And then five years ago, after the Uncle had died and the will was mired in the probate courts, cousin Collier had risen from the grave and contested it.

What exactly did she feel now, she wondered. Not guilt: her cousin's strange antics scarcely warranted it. Happiness, she decided—something of the same happiness she saw at this very moment on Eddie and Cleo's faces. She returned from her meanderings when she heard Langdon ask, "And so this man Collier Bonnet, who laid claim to the house—he's an imposter?"

"In some sense an imposter, yes," Bayhew answered, "but only in that his suicide turned out to have been staged. He is who he claims to be." Mr. Bayhew's steady demeanor, somber clothing, and iron-grey hair gave him a solid, unimaginative appearance— exactly what one wanted in a solicitor. "He provided documents proving his ancestry, and he unaccountably possessed a copy of Godfrey Walton's first will, which had bequeathed him half of the estate. The second will, however, written a year after the first, obviated its predecessor, and Bonnet inherited nothing at all. Bonnet's claim against the estate was quite without merit. He hired a Scottish attorney to represent him, and the attorney spewed out challenges and writs and stays until the young man was reduced to beggary. Put simply, Bonnet gambled everything on a bad hand of cards."

"Was there *nothing* for cousin Collier?" Alice asked. "I was fond of him when I was a girl. We were playmates, you know."

"Not a groat," Bayhew told her. "These strange capers that he cut—failing to die when he insisted he *had* died, and then

leaping out of the shadows when he smelled money... No, ma'am, he was too whimsical by half to be taken seriously by the courts. No doubt he had staged his death in order to escape criminal prosecution, or perhaps unhappy creditors, and then restored himself to life when he saw his chance to profit from it. If Godfrey Walton had died intestate, it might have gone differently for Collier Bonnet, but Godfrey Walton's intentions were clear. He gave the house and all within it to you, ma'am."

"Hurrah!" Cleo shouted, suddenly wide-awake, and Finn Conrad raised his mug and proposed a toast, which they all drank with great good will.

"There is one peculiar element, however," Bayhew said. "The house has supposedly been empty these many years, and I was worried that it had fallen in upon itself. I have an associate in Margate who acquiesced to look at it for me. I'm happy to say that the house is in good repair, although, my associate found it occupied."

"Occupied!" Gilbert said. "By whom? Squatters I don't doubt."

"Not apparently," Bayhew said. "A single gentleman lived there who claimed to be paying rent on the place, and has been for close onto three years. His name is Truelove, Baron Truelove, which you'll agree strikes a spurious note."

"A baron in what sense?" St. Ives asked. "A peerage?"

"No, a merely foreign appellation. I looked into the man's past and discovered that he spent time in France where he developed a reputation in what might be called the magical arts. The title that he assumed has no relevance in England, although he's keen on being addressed as if it were relevant—part of his... *costume,* if you take my meaning."

"Not entirely," St. Ives said. "A literal costume?"

"That of a mesmerist, God help us. He goes about dressed in gaudy robes and cloaks, lecturing on animal magnetism, magnetic fluid, and the magnetic contact with the dead—one of Madame Blavatsky's circle in London. There's nothing against him, mind you, in a legal sense—nothing that damns him outright—and he might be entirely innocent if one allows that a man has a right to believe in his own nonsense."

"It seems cheeky that he's living in the house under false circumstances," Gilbert said. "Tubby and I will pitch him out for you, Alice, his robes and cloaks into the bargain."

Mr. Bayhew blinked at Gilbert, as if wondering whether the old man was jesting.

"I have no grudge against robes and cloaks, Gilbert," Alice said. "Think of our neighbor Mother Laswell and her friends."

"Mother Laswell has proven her worth six times over," Gilbert said. "This Baron Truelove has not."

"We'll refrain from doing any pitching, Alice, unless you ask us to," Tubby said. "Uncle is being zealous. The iced pudding has quite likely frozen his brain." He winked at Eddie and Cleo.

Bayhew cleared his throat meaningfully. "In fact the Baron showed my associate a lease agreement allowing him tenancy," he said, "his third such document, renewed yearly."

"Signed by whom?" St. Ives asked.

"A Mr. Samuel Pickwick."

"Hah!" Gilbert exclaimed. "And this baronical idiot had no notion that the name was fraudulent? Pickwick indeed!"

Bayhew shrugged. "He was apparently happy with the transaction and did not see fit to contest small matters. Such a thing is relatively common, of course. An unscrupulous person sees that a dwelling sits empty, discovers that the owner is dead, and undertakes to lease it out, taking a year's rent money and providing a contract that he has no right to provide and which he signs with a false name. He then disappears, returning twelve months later to take another year's rent if no one has cried foul. My man in Margate was satisfied that some such thing had occurred, and that the Baron had in a sense been swindled—except, of course, that he had been residing in the house, and so the swindle was his good fortune."

"I'd bet a fiver that Samuel Pickwick is Collier Bonnet," St. Ives said.

Bayhew nodded. "He might well be. Bonnet would know absolutely that the house was empty and would know the circumstances surrounding it. And he assumed that the house might someday belong to him, which would give the whole thing the appearance of legitimacy and would allow him to rationalize his misdeeds, which in time mightn't be misdeeds at all. We could perhaps insist that the rents he collected be paid over to Mrs. St. Ives, if we knew where Bonnet resided and if the Baron was willing to testify that Bonnet was Pickwick. Conceivably Bonnet could be tracked down."

"We'll let Collier Bonnet go in peace," Alice said. "He *is* my own cousin, after all, and he is already the victim of his own foolishness. It's our good fortune that the house has been occupied. We'd find it full of bats and badgers otherwise."

"Of course," said St. Ives. "You're in the right of it, Alice. We've every reason to be thankful and no reason to ruin our good luck by casting stones at the unlucky."

"In any event this Baron Truelove was advised that he must remove himself," Bayhew said, casting a glance in Gilbert's direction. "So there should be no need to pitch anyone out. I posted a letter to that effect as soon as my man reported to me."

"And has he since taken himself away?" asked Alice.

"I do not know, ma'am, I'm sorry to say. This is all a very recent development."

"We'll hasten him along if he has not," Gilbert said, "pitching or no pitching. Tubby, you've brought your cudgel, I suppose? We'll tickle his ear with it until he laughs out of the other side of his mouth."

Bayhew affected not to have heard him, but produced a piece of foolscap from his case. "I've brought along a document that authorizes the police to remove him at your behest if he has not yet removed himself," Bayhew said to Alice. "The *police*, I say"— this with a glance at Gilbert. "At worst he will prove a short-lived irritation, since the law is quite clear on the matter. The house is yours, ma'am, and to my mind you should take possession of it whenever you choose to do so." With that he reached into his vest pocket and produced a pair of identical iron keys, which he placed on the table next to Alice's coffee mug.

"Well, well," Gilbert said. "I suggest that we ride down in the morning in my coach. We don't want the inimitable Baron to cart away the silver plate and the furnishings while we stand and wait."

....

SNARTLEGOG

lice discovered that she was unable to sleep, what with the celebratory wine, the late night food, and the feast of information that went with it. The world was quiet out beyond the open window, and she could see the stars above the tree line. She made out the Big Dipper, standing on end, having poured out its contents into the ocean. The window faced east, where, some forty miles as the crow flew, *Seaward* looked out on the same stars and onto that same ocean.

She returned to her reading, a section of her journal written in the summer of 1867, which had resided these past years in a trunk. It was a breathless account of the stranding of a sperm whale on the sands of Lazarus Bay, above which *Seaward* sat at the base of the chalk cliffs. The journal was bound in leather with a brass clasp, the margins of the paper decorated with drawings. She had measured the whale's length with a piece of line—sixty-three feet and six inches

long, according to what she had written in the journal—and the sketch in the margin was meant to show its immense height, nearly four times as high as the small Alice who stood next to it. Her uncle had promised her a tooth, which they would hack out of the jaw. Then they would blow-up the whale with dynamite before it stank too badly.

She had sat up late that long-ago night, watching the whale's body in the moonlight, the waves washing around it, shifting its great tail back and forth across the flooded beach, the moonlight glinting on its enormous eye. Finally she had fallen asleep to the sound of a rising storm and the hammering of breakers on the reef. As if by magic, the beach was empty when she awakened the next morning—no dynamite needed, thank heaven—the whale having been washed out to sea and swallowed up. She had no tooth to remember it by, only ink and paper.

She had dreamt about it regularly for years, however, the whale rising from the depths of her sleeping mind. There was something terrible about her whale dreams, and something grand—the ocean in its dark enormity: a vastness in which a giant whale was a mere piece of flotsam. There was a part of her that was happy—more than happy—with the comfort and security of Aylesford Village and its environs and in her homely life sheltered by hedgerows and tame woods and ponds and familiar faces. But there was another part of her that missed the ocean and the dreams that it engendered.

The downstairs clock began to toll, announcing midnight, and when it stopped she heard Langdon's tread on the stairs, he having sorted out what they would need for their hastily

conceived trip to the coast. The Frobishers had promised to call upon them at eight o'clock sharp.

"You're awake, then?" Langdon asked, sliding into bed beside her, already dressed in his nightshirt. In that moment a nightjar landed on the windowsill, a large beetle wiggling helplessly in its beak. The bird stood very still, illuminated by the small half-moon.

Alice poked Langdon lightly with her elbow and pointed toward the window, where the bird stood for another few moments before flying off. "Did you note the beetle in its beak?" she asked.

"A May beetle, I believe. It's rather late in the summer for a May beetle."

"Snartlegogs, my father called them. They're good bait for a hungry pike."

"I'd eat a snartlegog if I were a pike," St. Ives said. "Or even a carp."

"Shall I tell you about my uncle Godfrey?" she asked.

"Please do so. I have no good idea of the man." He sat up beside her and arranged his pillow behind his back. The breeze moved the bed curtains, and there was the ratcheting sound of a corncrake calling somewhere out in the night.

"Uncle Godfrey had lived at *Seaward* for years when Aunt Agatha first took me to meet him and my cousin Collier, whom I'd also merely heard of. I have a clear recollection of all of it, although I was perhaps six years old at the time. Uncle was a strange man, to be sure. I never felt that he was a threat, at least not to me. Indeed, he never touched me."

"Why should he have *touched* you? Do you mean indecently?"

"I suppose I do in a sense, although never at *all*, actually, not even to shake my hand. He beat Collier with a stick on several occasions—quite viciously. Collier would have tried the patience of an angel. Uncle Godfrey was a brooding man, and I cannot recall his ever having smiled. Certainly he never laughed. He went about his secret business and left the two of us to run wild as long as we kept away from locked rooms. This admonition incited Collier to do the opposite. He was forever going on about what might be found in those rooms, and that led to the beatings."

"Running wild was my favorite occupation as a child," Langdon said. "I availed myself of every opportunity to do so. I'm intrigued by your uncle's 'secret business.' Any particulars that you recall?"

"Not really," she said after a moment's hesitation. "It was evident that he had put up a wall, figuratively speaking, to hide things that we had no right to know, and from time to time I saw him in the company of men whose appearance frightened me. Collier invented dark secrets for him, but Collier's inventiveness was something like an illness. Some of it was probably true, however.

"In later years Uncle Godfrey became the skeleton that the family kept in the closet. There had been a scandal, and he had abruptly fallen out of favor. He was never again spoken of aloud by my parents, at least not in my hearing. There were whisperings—rumors of smuggling and other dark crimes that couldn't be named. Over time my curiosity evaporated. I missed *Seaward*, however, even though I didn't much miss Uncle Godfrey."

"You've no need to miss *Seaward* any longer."

"No, which makes me happy. And yet I find it impossible to sleep. Everything has changed on the instant. Do you feel that, also?"

"Something like that, certainly. Life seems to be settled, and then it's shaken apart, for better or worse. In this case I'm optimistic, unlike the poor snartlegog, whose luck failed him abruptly."

"Don't say such a thing," Alice told him. "It's foolish to boast about luck."

CHAPTER Four

....

THE MESMERIST

J ulian Hobbes sat in a chair, bound at the wrists and
ankles, his head slumped forward dejectedly, his coat,
vest, and shirt having been removed. They had taken
him to a makeshift cellar, a room cut into the chalk, and
he could see moonlight shining on the ocean through a
barred window. The night breeze carried the sea wind into
the room, and he was shivering with both cold and fear, his
brain aching and confused.

"This man St. Ives," Southerleigh asked. "What do you
know of him, Baron?"

"That he is a member of the Royal Society and the
Explorers Club. He studied at Edinburgh where he taught
for a brief period of time, and, to use the common phrase,
he is a jack-of-all-trades when it comes to the sciences—an
amateur mycologist, paleontologist, a student of the arcane,
and—philosophically—a libertarian in his way, a free-
thinker, not a libertine. We find his name associated with

dirigible flight, longevity serums, electro-magnetism, alleged time travel and space travel among many other things. His mind is enabled by a variety of brilliance, without a shadow of a doubt. And he is a do-gooder of the first water, although he does not put himself forward. He retired some few years back to Aylesford Village and set up as a gentleman farmer, his wife being moderately well-to-do and quite beautiful into the bargain. A formidable woman. Underestimate either of them at your peril."

A table, sculpted from the chalk and shining with a heavy coating of varnish, stood adjacent to the nearby wall, and on it sat a tray containing a pair of syringes filled with a murky fluid. A litter of mesmeric accoutrements lay beside the tray: magnets of varied sizes and shapes, colored spectacles, copper tubes, spritzers containing variously colored fluids, unset jewels and polished stones. Larsen and Forbes sat on wooden chairs, watching the procedure.

"Libertarian, forsooth," Larsen put in now, somewhat past sober. "In other words, this St. Ives is a self-invented fraud. He shores himself up with empty-headed philosophies and pays for it with his wife's fortune. He's a damned hugger mugger, it seems to me." He winked at the unhappy Hobbes, belched heavily, and drank off the dregs of his wine, smacking his lips and reaching again for the bottle, which he discovered was empty.

"No, sir, the man is not a fraud of any variety," the Baron said. "He was instrumental in bringing down Jules Klingheimer in London. You do recall Jules Klingheimer, Larsen?"

"Not willingly."

"There was little of it in the newspapers because St. Ives avoids public display and has friends at *The Times* who purposely downplay his exploits. At the time of the Klingheimer affair he was aided by a band of unlikely confederates, and the lot of them slipped away unseen after knocking a great number of chess pieces off the board. Even more telling is that St. Ives has been of particular interest to Dr. Ignacio Narbondo for *many* years, the good doctor failing to rid the world of Professor St. Ives on several occasions. Indeed, it is rumored that St. Ives might have ridded the world of Narbondo during the murky affair of the Glass Cathedral in Blackfriars some time ago. Narbondo was known to have been present at that debacle, and he has not been seen since. His house in Blackfriars sits empty."

"Please describe St. Ives, Baron," Southerleigh said. "I want to know him when I see him."

"Two inches over six feet tall, perhaps thirteen stone. That's close enough. He's fit—not bookish. Hollow cheeks. Rugged looking, one might say—craggy. Dark hair, although perhaps running to grey these days. I'll add that he is familiar with the use of the shillelagh and can break your jaw before you know it. I've seen him speak on two occasions at the Royal Society, in one of the large rooms at Burlington House."

"You haven't met the man?"

"No, and just as well."

"Indeed," Southerleigh said, and right then Hobbes began to shake as if stricken with palsy, his teeth clacking together violently. "Settle my cape around Mr. Hobbes's shoulders if you will, Jensen," the Baron said. "I fear that he is on the verge of

being carried away by a fit. Quickly now. Give him a good whiff of the smelling salts."

And then to Hobbes, whose head snapped back onto his shoulders when the vial of salts was waved beneath his nostrils, the Baron said, "I adjure you to remain calm, sir. You need have no fears whatsoever. It is true that you'll be delayed in your return to Canterbury, and your father will quite likely be disappointed of your mother's so-called Death Book, but you've everything to gain by composing yourself. The success of this—this *experiment*—depends upon it."

"Baron," Southerleigh said, "We'll offer the St. Ives woman twice the lease we're currently paying for the house. If she refuses, we'll treble it, but pretend to be shrewd in your negotiations so as not to put them on alert."

"Capital idea. My sense of things entirely."

"And what of the pitiful Pickwick?"

"He has absconded, to the best of my knowledge," the Baron said. "Wisely, I must say."

"I'm not at all certain that he has. I believe he is lurking hereabouts and that we can reel him back in."

"Certainly, if that is the will of the Society," the Baron said. "I'm indifferent to the man."

"Not I," Forbes put in. "He is guilty of violating several of the Articles, after all, and who knows what other crimes he has committed against us, including misrepresenting his ownership of the house on Lazarus Bay."

"Yes," Southerleigh said. "But we have more immediate things to attend to, Mr. Forbes. Delicate things. Pickwick is a

born fool. Mr. Hobbes is not. We must turn our minds to the shipment to Calais."

"As for our friend Mr. Hobbes, we're now quite ready," the Baron said.

He selected a prepared syringe from the tray on the table, and then wrapped a strand of india-rubber around Hobbes's upper arm, knotting it tightly. After a moment's waiting he jabbed the heavy needle into Hobbes's forearm and depressed the piston, the liquid within taking a full minute to flow out of the syringe, the pain of the operation evident on Hobbes's face. Forbes stood up out of his chair, moving beside Larsen to watch the fun.

Hobbes attempted to swing his head sideways now, his teeth gnashing in an effort to bite the Baron's forearm, but Jensen yanked Hobbes's head upright again and held him tightly.

"Struggling will avail you nothing," the Baron said in what was meant as a compassionate voice. He gazed steadily into Hobbes's stricken face while slowly removing a watch from his own breast pocket. He glanced at the watch and then, renewing his gaze into Hobbes's eyes, he said, "You must put yourself at ease, Mr. Hobbes. Somnambulism is quite a pleasant experience, a journey into the recesses of your own thoughts, which will shortly be released from agitation. Untroubled. Easy. Serene.

"I want you to open your mind to me, and when I've peered into it, I will close the door on it again, and you will have only the haziest recollection of this experience. Imagine yourself in a boat on a river, a placid river, lapping against green mead-ows on either side, cloud-drift in the blue sky. Silence descends

roundabout you, and you can hear the music of the spheres, the moons and planets turning in harmony in the skies…"

He glanced at the watch again. A shudder ran through Hobbes's body, and he stiffened in his chair, a stony rictus overtaking his features, his mouth turning downward with such force that his cheeks appeared skeletal. His eyes were pried open by an invisible force working within him. He began to shake uncontrollably, spittle running out of either side of his mouth, and he would have tumbled out of the chair if he weren't strapped in.

The Baron slapped him lightly on the cheek, and in an even voice said, "*Attend* to me, Mr. Hobbes. *Attend* to me, I say. Your boat drifts upon the river. You see the water beneath you—a shifting green clarity, waterweeds swaying in the current, the passing clouds reflected on the surface. You *are* the river, Mr. Hobbes, you are *of* the river, you…"

Hobbes stiffened now as if electrocuted, and he opened his mouth until it seemed as if his face would split. The Baron stepped back hastily, pushing Southerleigh out of the way with his forearm as Hobbes, his head abruptly lashing on his neck, vomited a blood-tinged gush of dark fluid, ejecting it with such force that it splashed against the far wall. Larsen and Forbes hindered each other in their efforts to stand aside, but a second vomitous blast hosed both of them down, and Larsen vomited in turn, splashing Southerleigh's shoes even though the Baron and Southerleigh had retreated to the window, where they stood gulping in draughts of the sea air against the foul, winey reek within the room.

Hobbes collapsed utterly, and Jensen pinched both his cheeks in an effort to call him back. He yanked Hobbes's ears, shouted into them, and then once again waved the smelling salts under his nose, jamming it against the nostrils.

"It's useless," the Baron said after another minute had gone by. He felt for a pulse and shook his head in defeat. "The man had a weak constitution. He's beyond recovery. Hang the corpse, Jensen, and bleed the body, and then throw his innards to the dogs, unless the members would rather make a sausage of them. Forbes, what do you say to a sausage?"

Larsen vomited again, and the Baron laughed aloud.

"Put his corpse on ice," Southerleigh said, "and we'll endeavor to sell his head to the French."

"When do we sail?" the Baron asked.

"Soon, Baron. Soon." He collected himself, and said, "Shouldn't we perhaps call the members for a Friday supper party? There's virtue in Mr. Hobbes's flesh, even a dead Hobbes, if he remains suitably iced."

"Ah, the members and their appetites!" the Baron said. "Do as you will. Let us not forget the matter of my fee, however, which I will collect on the morrow. I intend to remove myself to London if the St. Ives woman elects to remain in the house. This has been a profitable interlude for the both of us, but I fear that the ice is getting thin, and I have no wish to fall through it."

CHAPTER Five

SEAWARD

Gilbert Frobisher's coach-and-four carried its passengers around a sharp bend on the Cliff Road a half-mile below the North Foreland Light. An ancient yew tree, which marked the steep entrance to Lazarus Bay and the far northern verge of Alice's property, came into view on the left hand some distance ahead. Its immense limbs had shaded the Cliff Road for two centuries, or so her uncle had told Alice when she had first visited *Seaward*.

The town of Broadstairs lay another mile beyond Lazarus Bay. Everyone except Finn Conrad intended to stay in town at the Royal Albion Hotel; Finn would bunk at *Seaward* in the spirit of adventure. Alice was happy to stay in the hotel, for the trip out from Aylesford had been wearying after last night's festivities, and the old house would certainly want civilizing. Tomorrow they would haul in food and other necessities, air the house, and determine whether the mice had nibbled the bed linens or bats had invaded

the upper floors. There was much to be done, and although she missed Eddie and Cleo, she was happy to have four days clear before the children would arrive.

Boggs, Gilbert's coachman, reined in the horses now, slowing down and fixing the skid plate against the wheel as they edged around onto the flat-cobbled path that descended into the cove. Wave-washed reefs ran diagonally out to sea from the near end, the waves diminishing as they entered the deep, comparatively calm water farther along to the south, where the rocky shingle was buried under a wide swath of sand. The sun glittering on the surface of the sea lent it a falsely cheerful appearance, and the noise of the waves breaking across the headland grew louder as the coach descended. Alice marveled at the notion that the deserted expanse of seaweed-strewn beach belonged to her—to the family, of course—as well as a good deal of the wooded land on the bluffs above.

"There it is: *Seaward*," Alice said to Finn when the three-level shingled house appeared before them, standing near the base of the cliff. It nestled in a broad cut in the chalk that had been widened by ages of run-off from the wooded heights. Three distinct sections of black slate roof stepped downwards toward the sea, with broad eaves that made the roofs appear to float. She counted the eight chimneys, thinking of the lorry-loads of coal and wood it took to warm the house and heat the stove the year around, all of which would have to be hauled in from Margate. She thought about the winter storms, the gales of howling wind, the vast breakers beating the shore, the driving rain, the rills of water cascading from the cliff, and the occasional lumps of

chalk hurtling down. It was a darkly romantic place to be sure, but not a leisurely place.

"Do you see the high rock wall that stands behind the house?" she asked Finn. "It's meant as a barrier to falling pieces of chalk. The pink and yellow flowers growing upon it are creeping sea fig. My uncle had me pickle the figs, which he ate as a relish, but I couldn't abide them."

"What lies beyond the wall?" Finn asked. "I see what looks to be a ladder leading up the cliff."

"So it does. It must have been put up after my time here. Cousin Collier and I climbed fissures in the cliff itself as a short-cut to the woods."

"The ladder makes it a quicker bolt-hole, maybe, if someone has to cut and run. Someone who's not nimble, so to say. I'll just take a look at it, if I may, when there's time."

"You may take a look at whatever suits you, Finn, and your time is yours to spend. I'm aware that looking into things is your particular passion. And so I'll point out that there's a trapdoor in the storage room off the kitchen that leads to a downward sloping tunnel into a sea cave. You'd find the door on your own, I dare say, under the rug, and so I'll tell you that the sea cave is dangerous at high tide, which rises quickly along this part of the coast. I've seen the beach utterly washed away in a storm, and then tons of sand replaced afterward in a few day's time."

The coach drew to a stop, and Alice looked for a gig or a wagon that might belong to the mysterious Baron. She was happy not to see any such thing. As if in silent agreement they

sat for a moment gazing at the high, blue-painted door, the color faded by weather, the heavy timbers lined with cracks.

"It's changed its character during my time away," Alice said in a low voice, as if talking to herself.

"How-so?" Langdon asked.

"I can scarcely explain. Perhaps it's me who's changed. It's become a sort of ghost. Can you make out the figures hidden in the shingles below the eaves?—the image of a man carrying a bundle of sticks on the left of the attic window and the quarter moon looking through a cloud on the right?"

"Now that you point the figures out, yes."

"They were the same blue as the door when I was a girl, not faded as they are now. I have the strangest notion that they're simply disappearing, like a memory."

"Not a bit of it," Gilbert said. "A new coat of paint will spiff the place up. Paint is the answer to most of the world's ills, Alice. I have myself *gilded* from time to time, you know, to maintain my vast and shining beauty."

"God save us," Tubby muttered, as his uncle laughed aloud at his own nonsense. Boggs, having climbed down from his seat, swung the door open, and Tubby gallantly handed Alice down to him before clambering down heavily himself, Finn and St. Ives following behind. Gilbert descended last, the carriage rising upon its springs at the sudden lightening of the load.

Alice stepped into the shade of the portico and produced the iron keys from her handbag. She fitted one of them into the lock, turned it, and opened the door, peering into the dim house before crossing the threshold into the entry hall and drawing

room. She drew back the heavy curtains, sunshine pouring through the dimpled and striated old glass. The house was as Alice remembered—the same massive, dark furniture with deep seats and thick cushions, comfortable rather than elegant, but somewhat sinister. The stone fireplace was cavernous, with and-irons in the shape of glass-eyed gargoyles and with high-backed, cushioned settles standing on either side.

"Here's a stuffed peccary waiting on the landing, by God!" Gilbert called out. "Finn, have you ever laid eyes on a peccary? The Americans call them skunk pigs. They're one of God's little jokes. Look at the beady eyes and the tiny legs. They have no idea that they're amusing."

"Nor have others of us," Tubby said, peering at the titles of the books in a glass-fronted book-case.

Alice considered the smoke-dimmed painting that hung over the deep mantle—a burning city sending a wild reek into a black, night sky, tormented faces whirling skyward in the smoke, the frail human figures fleeing away, Lot's wife looking back in horror at Sodom in flames. The painting had been little more than a curiosity to her as a girl, but it was disturbing now. She had the strange notion that the passing years had fallen away in an instant, and that she was in fact two persons in one—a girl and a woman: this was not quite the house that she had visited as a girl, nor was she the girl who had visited the house.

"Perhaps we can find a more suitable painting to hang over the mantelpiece," Langdon said, coming up to stand beside her.

"I can't help but wonder why Lot's wife had no name," Alice said to him. "The Bible is full of names, after all. Nor have I ever

understood why looking back was such a crime. Her life, after all, had gone up in flames, quite literally. The people she knew were dead, or soon would be. Of course she looked back. Why was she turned into a pillar of salt?"

"An admonition to do as one is told to do, perhaps."

"Told to do? By a suddenly appearing man who claims to be an angel? I'm skeptical. Perhaps the pillar of salt business is another of God's little jokes, like Gilbert's skunk-pig."

She walked to the base of the broad stairway that led to the second and third levels, standing beside Gilbert and the peccary. There were sconces set into niches in the stairway walls, with the familiar fat beeswax candles sitting in them and a box that held Lucifer matches and a scissors to trim the candlewicks. She was fond of the honeyed smell of burning beeswax, which perfumed the air of the room at this very moment.

"I believe that there are candles burning above," she said in a low voice.

Gilbert, hearing something in her tone, moved out of sight behind the settles flanking the hearth, jerking his head at Tubby, who followed him. Finn had already disappeared into the kitchen.

Alice and Langdon ascended the stairs, and within six winding steps upward, Alice saw the glow of burning candles and a descending shadow on the stairway.

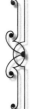

CHAPTER Six

HER UNCLE'S DOMAIN

A man appeared and stood looking down upon them—tall and heavy-framed. His face, half illuminated by a candle-flame, appeared to have been chiseled out of a stone quarry. His long white hair was swept back under a high collar, and his dark eyes regarded them without expression for a moment before his visage became somewhat more human, as if by an act of will.

"I did not expect you so soon," he said, bowing from his shoulders. "I am the Baron Truelove." He wore a cape, a leather hat with a wide brim, a silver buckle on his belt, and Hessian boots with more silver buckles—altogether as if he were dressed for a production at Drury Lane.

"I am Alice St. Ives, Baron, and I'm afraid that I've inherited this house out from under you. This is my husband, Langdon St. Ives."

The Baron stepped downward, holding out his hand, which Alice shook, Langdon following suit. The man

seemed cordial enough, but Alice was struck with the notion there was something off about him. She had no prejudices against theatrical clothing, certainly clothes did not "make the man," as the tired old proverb went. So what was it? Gilbert's suspicions had seeped into her mind, perhaps. Or perhaps the Baron's air of playacting struck a false note that his bluff demeanor couldn't hide.

"We've come to take possession of my wife's property," Langdon said cheerfully.

"Of *course*, sir. Here is the key—my sole copy, although I'll warn you that my self-styled landlord, a man who goes by the name of Pickwick, possesses another. I've been informed that the man is a ne'er-do-well."

"Was he a tall, thin man by any chance?" Alice asked. "Red hair?"

"That's the fellow. I doubt that we'll see him again on earth. You'll be happy to hear that I've decamped to Broadstairs, where I'm remaining temporarily with a friend. My man will arrive shortly with the wagon to carry the remainder of my luggage, and I'll take my leave."

"We'll help you cart your possessions downstairs," Alice told him. "I'm very sorry to rout you out on short notice, and even more sorry that this alleged Pickwick abused your trust."

The Baron looked from one to the other of them as if considering his words before going on. "I would like for you to grant me a boon, ma'am. I desire to lengthen my stay here at *Seaward*. I'm afraid that I'm a sore imposition on the friend I'm currently staying with, a solitary old gentleman who values his routine,

hidebound, if you follow me. I have four months left on my admittedly spurious lease—twenty pounds worth of days."

"You'll be happy to hear that we've filled out a cheque in your name on the advice of our solicitor," Langdon said. He reached into his vest pocket and removed the cheque, handing it to the Baron.

"I assure you that the money is secondary," the Baron said. "Here now. You've made it out for twenty-five quid, and I'm afraid that I have no money about my person. I'll hazard a bold request: I'll return this to you and happily pay you twice the sum if you'd simply allow me to remain here for a short time. I'm engaged in Maidstone until the end of September, do you see."

"Alas, the thing is impossible," Alice said. "We, too, are engaged in the area, as you put it. Mr. Bayhew, our solicitor, informs us that you were sent a legal notice to vacate the premises."

"I received the notice, certainly. But will you not consider my request, ma'am?"

"I'm sorry to say that I cannot," Alice said. "I find explanations tiresome, and further conversation would change nothing."

"If I were to *treble* the figure, ma'am? One hundred pounds for a three-months reprieve, let us say? A nicely round sum."

"It won't do," Langdon told him, no longer smiling.

Alice put her hand on her husband's arm. "We're terribly sorry, Baron. But our children are *very* keen on joining us once we've settled in. We mean to resort here off and on into the autumn."

"Waste not a moment, eh?" the Baron said, smiling widely. "I very much understand. I believe I hear my man Jensen now."

There was the rattle of a wagon drawing up outside, and it occurred to Alice that their own arrival in Gilbert's coach must have produced even more of a racket, and that the Baron might easily have been lurking on the stairs, listening to their conversation.

"I'll just fetch my possessions, then," the Baron said, and with that he stepped away toward the upper stories.

"We insist on lending a hand," Langdon told him, and he and Alice followed him into the top floor of the house—her uncle's domain, utterly forbidden to Alice when she was a girl. There was a wide landing at the top, with hallways running along in either direction, each with several doors. Cousin Collier, having managed to open some of these doors, had told her that they held her uncle's "collections," which he had gathered from far parts of the world. She remembered her uncle's outrage when he discovered that Collier had taken a wax impression of the key that opened them. Collier refused to tell Alice what he had seen, although whether his refusal had to do with his fear of a second beating, or with some other horror, she had never known. Perhaps tomorrow she would look into them.

The Baron unlocked a door dead center of the landing that led into what had been her uncle's domain. The room beyond was vast, with only one interior door, open now, beyond which stood a water closet. There was a heavily draped bed and other pieces of bed-chamber-type furniture gathered together in one corner: a sleeping quarters mostly hidden by folding screens carved with depictions of sea creatures. The rest of the room was cluttered with a number of wardrobes and library tables from the middle of the last century.

Lining the walls were cases and cases of books, many of them apparently ancient. Alcoves separated the bookcases, each alcove hung with a painting or bearing an object, including several age-darkened skulls and also primitive weapons—vicious looking clubs set with boar tusks or ebony spikes. She looked at the nearest painting and was unhappy to see that it depicted a jungle clearing in which savages were flaying the bare chest of a man who lay upon a table. There was a black kettle nearby and a fire lit beneath it. Severed body parts lay in the grass below the table.

"I found these paintings quite…unsettling," the Baron said, looking at Alice, whose face no doubt betrayed her own feelings. "And as for many of the books…" He shook his head darkly. "It was none of my business to put any of it out of sight, and I was careful not to meddle with it despite my private inclinations, which have everything to do with the elevation of life, physical and spiritual, rather than…"

He gestured dismissively and his smile reappeared. "Here now," he said, picking up his two portmanteaus from the floor, one in either hand. "I'm taking along that crate of my own books, lying there by the fireplace fender." St. Ives stepped across and picked it up. "Dull spiritual texts, I'm afraid," the Baron said of the boxed books. "I find that they keep my soul plumb, level, and square, to borrow a phrase from the Freemasons, and certainly they help me to fall asleep at night."

And with that the Baron and Langdon, carrying the crate of books, set out down the stairs. Alice stood for a moment, surveying the room now that it was empty of the Baron's irritating

presence. Her uncle, even in death, cast a dark shadow over a piece of her family history, and this room, his private quarters, was the cupboard that contained his skeleton, to use the old phrase. She wondered at Collier having given the Baron the run of the house. The Collier Bonnet she knew would have been more circumspect about the terms of the lease. Perhaps it was his way of repaying their uncle for the thrashing that he had received after having been caught snooping in this very room. Then it occurred to her that Collier Bonnet might not have set the terms of the lease.

That notion was followed close on by the now obvious fact that the Baron had surely been waiting for their arrival, no doubt to ask them outright to allow him to remain in the house. Except that he could not have known they would arrive today at all, which meant that he had never really vacated the house despite Bayhew's letter advising him to do so, and despite the nonsense about his having walked down from Broadstairs this very day.

Happily, the Baron was taking his leave by the time she descended the stairs. He was standing outside now, and Langdon and Tubby stood just inside the doorway, as if ready to block his way should he attempt to rush back in. The Baron's footman, a hulking simian who looked very much like a Seven Dials thug, was just then settling the portmanteaus and the books onto the bed of the wagon. The Baron bowed, climbed onto the seat, and within moments the wagon was laboring uphill toward the road.

....

CHAPTER Seven

PICKWICK'S LENDING LIBRARY

The ladder up the chalk had fifty-six rungs, and Finn had scrambled up the tilted face at something like a run while he counted them, finding himself upon a landing floored with rough-cut planks, no doubt meant to be less slippery than the chalk in wet weather. Sitting on this perch he took in his surroundings through a small, collapsing telescope, and he watched the Baron's wagon climb away up the hill toward the road until it disappeared out of sight. The sky over the ocean was dark with clouds, hurrying toward shore, the end of the sunny afternoon. Almost certainly there was a storm rising.

He stood up, thinking to explore the woods, but immediately hid behind an outcropping of chalk when he saw that a stranger stood a few feet from the top of the cliff some distance farther along, hidden in the shadows of the trees and studying the beach through binocular field glasses. Finn saw

that the Professor and the Frobishers had come out of the house and were heading toward the water's edge now. Gilbert pointed out to sea, apparently calling their attention to a never-ending line of seabirds flying in the direction of Margate.

Alice appeared on the beach now, wearing a hooded cape. She angled away from the men, strolling toward the exposed reefs at the northern edge of the cove, where sizeable swells rolled in, throwing over in a tumult of whitewater. The tide hadn't turned yet, and there was still a broad stretch of sand and shingle where the waves played themselves out.

The man with the field glasses seemed to be following Alice's progress in particular, and he set his instrument on the ground now and took from his coat pocket what appeared to be a cricket ball. He fiddled with it for a moment, threw his arm back, and lobbed it hard out over the beach. The ball descended, bounced off a large, smooth piece of white chalk half buried in the sand, and plunked down a few feet from where Alice stood, rolling past her. She stared at it for a moment and then stooped to pick it up, removing what was apparently a folded piece of foolscap tied to it with string. She turned to survey the cliffs, shading her face with her hand. But, Finn saw now, his man had quite disappeared.

Through his glass he watched a small, two-masted steamship that lay some distance offshore, its boiler and funnel amidships sending up a plume of black smoke that fled away on the wind. The ship sported a curious structure in the stern, like a small cabin with a lean-to roof, a crane visible rising above. The steamship, perhaps 80 feet in length, appeared to be anchored,

although surely it would have to get underway if it meant to ride out the coming storm or to find shelter.

Finn moved into the trees now, a sycamore glade with low-hanging limbs, where he hid behind a broad trunk. He saw the curious stranger again some twenty yards distant, the man standing beside a whimsical wagon, very much like a gypsy caravan, pulled by two pleasant looking Shetlanders or maybe Highland ponies. They were tethered to a tree that was part of a coppiced hedge, which hid the wagon from the view of anyone deeper in the woods. The wagon was gaily painted, with upward-swinging doors along the side. On the doors were painted the words "Pickwick's Lending Library."

The man pushed his field glasses in behind the seat of the wagon and then stood by the ponies, speaking to them and stroking their noses. Slipping his hand into a leathern bag tied to the side of the cart he drew out two apples, offering one to each, the ponies accepting the gifts happily.

Clearly he was Alice's scapegrace cousin Collier Bonnet, the self-styled Samuel Pickwick. It seemed both fabulous and appealing to Finn that the man drove a portable library. His friendliness to the ponies argued that he had a good heart. But just as this observation entered Finn's mind, Pickwick burst into a paroxysm of weeping and began to tear at his hair as if to yank it out. Abruptly he ceased his antics and put his hand to his ear, and then rushed to the far end of the hedge and peeked out in the direction of the Cliff Road, which cut through the woods beyond.

There was the sound of a conveyance of some sort coming along, and within moments, the Baron's wagon appeared in

the distance, away through the trees, heading in the direction of Broadstairs. Pickwick stood immobile until the sound of the wagon had passed away, and then hurriedly untied the horses' tether, climbed up onto the seat, and set out in the direction of the road, turning north toward Margate.

"DESCRIBE HIM TO ME if you will," Alice said to Finn. Langdon and the Frobishers already sat within Gilbert's coach, and the door stood open, Boggs waiting to hand her in.

"A red-haired man, gangly thin, driving a caravan that said "Pickwick's Lending Library" on the side. He threw the cricket ball from the top of the cliff, like I said. I believe he was waiting in the woods for the Baron's wagon to pass by, as if he knew it was coming along and it wasn't safe to be seen on the road."

"And you're certain he was weeping? Not laughing or taken with a fit of coughing?"

"Yes, ma'am. He was took with a paroxysm, as they say."

She paused for a moment, thinking, and then said, "I believe I'll go into Margate tomorrow, Finn. Will you come along? We'll hire a wagon in Broadstairs so that the two of us can drive in together. I intend to fill the larder, for I mean to cook meals in this house just as soon as we've chased the ghosts out of it tomorrow. Perhaps we'll find a piece of furniture or two. I must tell you, however, that Langdon is off to Pegwell Bay tomorrow with the Frobishers in search of natterjack toads. Are you keen on going along on the toad hunt rather than into Margate?"

"No, ma'am. I'm happy to go into Margate with you regardless," Finn said. "I can catch up with them if I know where they'll be."

"Well, I value that. I have business with my cousin, who as you know is in a sad state. The letter tied to the stone was a summons. I'd be thankful were you nearby. Eight o'clock, let's say. There's a firm called Whitman's just off The Parade where we can secure a small wagon."

"I'll go into Broadstairs directly I'm awake," Finn said.

"And you feel secure spending the night here at *Seaward?*"

"Oh, yes, ma'am. I'll remember what you said about the cave, and I'll bundle the pictures up on the top floor into the big closet, unless you'd rather I burned them on the beach."

"Yes, do that very thing if you have time, Finn. Burn them to ashes. You've heard the proverb about the new broom that sweeps clean? We must sweep away the cobwebs and spiders and shadows. Until tomorrow morning then."

THE COACH SWEPT UP the hill at a determined clip, and Alice was filled with a curious mixture of elation and anger. She looked out over the sea, wondering about the Baron and about her uncle, the strange perversions that bent men got up to in pursuit of their hidden desires and odd predilections. She removed Bonnet's cricket ball note from her bag and read it aloud to her three companions:

"For the sake of our past together, meet me in the Sparrow Tavern at the base of the Cold Harbour stairs, Dear Alice. I'll wait there through the day if need be. Your servant, Collier Bonnet."

JAMES P. BLAYLOCK

"A summons," Gilbert said. "He's an audacious fellow, to be sure."

"He's badly frightened of something. It's the Baron, I believe, who is an audacious man. You were entirely in the right of it, Gilbert, when you warned us against him. I believe that he knew the identity of Pickwick all along, and he knew that the name on the lease would hide my cousin's actual name. Almost certainly it was the Baron himself who perpetuated the lease fraud. He put poor Collier up to it in order to assume a sort of ownership of *Seaward*."

"Perhaps it would be best if I bowed out of our collecting jaunt into Pegwell and went into Margate with you."

"Please do nothing of the sort. Finn has agreed to squire me into Margate in the morning. Collier would be shy if you were along. He won't regard Finn as a threat. I very much hope that he will make a clean breast of it, which will settle our differences."

The white chimneys of the Royal Albion Hotel came into sight now, and Gilbert and Tubby, the yeomen of food, began to discuss supper: deviled ham, oysters, Dover sole, lamb from the Romney Marsh along with new potatoes roasted in the drippings, a mountain of Stilton cheese afterward. Champagne, perhaps, to celebrate.

"I fancy steamed treacle pudding for dessert. With custard," Alice said, realizing that she was both desperately hungry and desperately happy. "It's a good house," she said to Langdon, placing her hand on his knee, "now that we've sent the Baron packing."

CHAPTER Eight

THE RISING STORM

Finn had collected the offensive paintings in order to have the burning done with enough daylight left to look into the sea cave, which would be better illuminated if there were still sunlight left, low in the sky. He had no particular reaction to the paintings aside from a vague uneasiness. They were much like illustrations from a book of adventures, except that there was something unclean about them. A person's eye went straight to the horrors, which were the only tale the pictures told. Certainly they would give Eddie and Cleo nightmares, and that was enough for him to burn them cheerfully.

He took it upon himself to look into various closets, where he discovered a half dozen small, framed pictures depicting the tortures of Hell being perpetrated on unclothed sinners. He carried these down as well, heaping them all into a barrow, deciding to leave the numerous skulls and several shrunken heads for further consideration. Finn had

nothing against them, quite the contrary, and the Professor might understand them to be scientific.

He hauled the heap down to a point below the line of seaweed and driftwood left by the last tide, where he tilted the paintings against each other to make a sort of teepee, which shuddered in the sea wind. After emptying a jar of lamp oil over the top of them, he struck a match, let it flare within his cupped hands, and tossed it in among the paintings. The fire raced up the old wooden frames, ignited the canvas, and the entire mass burst into such a high, leaping flame that he stepped away backward, astonished at the billowing smoke.

Within minutes the canvasses had blackened and curled, and the frames had begun to fall in upon themselves. The wind continued to fan the fire, and the entire lot burned to cinders—a hellish end to hellish paintings. The incoming tide would sweep the beach clean.

The surf had risen even further, and spectacular breakers were quartering across the reefs at the top end of the cove, the air full of spindrift. The southern sky was a mass of tearing clouds— dirty weather tonight, and fairly soon. He pushed the barrow back up the strand, stopping at the top of the incline to look out to sea where the low sun shone on the steamship that still lay in the offing. He wondered at the temerity of the Captain, anchoring so close to shore in a rising storm and no great distance from the Goodwin Sands. Finn had no time to stand and watch, however, for the sun was descending and the tide coming up fast.

Behind a heavy, plank door in the kitchen stood the room that Alice had mentioned, a musty smelling storage chamber

of cupboards and open shelves. Two coils of dirty rope hung on the wall, and an open keg of nails, gone to rust, sat on the floor along with equally rusty carpenter's tools, the lot of it cobwebby and disused. An old coracle built of willow rods and tarred hide, rotted through and no longer seaworthy, stood tilted into a corner along with its broad paddle. Five lanterns, two cans of lamp oil, and a tin matchbox sat on another shelf, these being newer and apparently more recently used.

A heavy rug covered the center of the floor, and Finn hauled it back to reveal the trapdoor. There was a wooden bar keeping it fixed, the bar and its iron hold-downs imbedded in the floor. The locking mechanism, a simple latch, was easy enough to unfasten, obviously meant to keep things from coming up from below, and he soon had the door tilted back on its hinges. A gust of spumey air blew into the room, carrying the fishy, weedy smell of the sea cave.

He took a lantern from the shelf, lit the wick, and stepped down a short flight of wooden stairs onto the sandy floor of the cavern proper, looking around to see how the excavation had been done, doubtless by smugglers. They had tunneled upward through the several feet of chalk, the pick marks evident in the chalk, and had built the storage room above to hide the opening—a perfect smuggler's lair. He wondered if Alice had twigged it when she was a girl, and whether her strange uncle was a smuggler himself or had bought the house after the days of smuggling had waned.

He walked beneath the beams that supported the ceiling and followed a narrowing tunnel downward, his lantern held

out ahead. The sandy floor had been cleared of rocks—easier to navigate in the dark—and soon he saw the glimmer of sunlight on the water pooled within the sea cave itself. Small waves rolled across the surface, murmuring over the exposed weeds and rocks, the hollow boom of breaking surf sounding in the distance. The cavern widened to form a little half-moon beach, which sloped upward on the left-hand side. Finn stood staring at what he saw back in the shadows, safely above the level of the pool and resting on a trestle of heavy timbers: a line of six-sided wooden boxes that appeared to be coffins, sitting on the skeleton frame of a bench.

He stepped across the rocks to the beach and shined the lantern on the coffins. They were newly built, that was clear, and each had a number burned into the foot-end, visible in the lantern glow: forty-three through forty-nine. He looked about himself and listened hard to make sure that he was quite alone, the notion of smugglers and potential corpses putting an edge on things. But who smuggled corpses? His mind turned on what might be inside the coffins if it wasn't corpses—more likely rifles, perhaps bottles of stolen spirits. A clever smuggler might stow anything in a coffin.

He wondered whether they were coming or going—hidden here on their way to London, perhaps. Atop the sixth coffin in line sat a box somewhat larger than a hat-box, covered in lead. The joints were sealed with solder, the number 50 stamped into the soft metal. Dangling from a nail at the end of the coffin was an envelope made of oiled silk, the edges sealed in wax. He wondered what he was looking at—the water-tight envelope, the

coffins, the lead box—nothing right and natural, that was sure, nothing on the up and up. A surge of whitewater washed into the cave behind him, reminding him of the time passing, and he berated himself for not having come into the cave sooner.

In for a penny, he thought, and yanked the envelope off its nail, considered it for a moment, and opened the wax seal. There was a sheet of paper inside—vellum, it seemed to him—marked with a wax pencil against the wet. It appeared to be a manifest, seven sets of letter pairs with spaces between, each with a number corresponding to a coffin: "43 WI ZA, 44 SA PI…" Code perhaps. The seventh and final—"5O JU HO," was as meaningless as the rest of it. At the bottom of the manifest was the word "destination" followed by "Eglise Notre-Dame, Calais." They were bound for a churchyard in France it would seem, as if for burial, although by a suspiciously circuitous route.

He grasped the corner of one of the coffins and attempted to raise it, but it was heavy, and he let it drop the inch or two back onto the timbers. A moment passed as he stood thinking, and during that moment there sounded a strange scrabbling noise within the box that he had shifted. His heart gave a lurch, and he stepped away instinctively, listening for something more but hearing only the muffled sound of the surf and the calling of gulls. Then it came again—a low, creaking sound this time, not quite human, but not quite anything else.

Leave, he told himself, but he waited to hear something more—a third time would be inarguable. He counted elephants, deciding to give it thirty, but then considered that if there were no further sounds it might mean that the person inside had

expired while Finn Conrad was counting elephants. All signs pointed to a living person trapped within—surely living.

The box, as was apparently true of the rest of them, had a hinged lid fixed with a hasp and lock. He set the papers with the lantern atop the adjacent box and grabbed up a piece of chalk, which he smashed down onto the lock, hammering away with two-handed blows, the fourth blow beating the hasp entirely free of the wood, so that the lock and hasp fell together into the sand.

Steeling himself, he raised the lid. A man lay within apparently dead, his lips pulled back so that his teeth were bared like those of an animal. His eyes were shut, but the eyeballs appeared to be moving behind the lids, as if he were asleep and not dead at all. A wave washed up the slope, wetting Finn's boots, the tide coming up fast now.

He heard the unmistakable sound of oars turning in rowlocks, and he snatched up the lantern and papers. Against the sunlit cave mouth, the shadow of a rowing boat was just then pulling into the mouth of the cave, six men rowing. He leapt across the beach in three strides, crossed the rocks along the pool's edge, and jumped onto the uphill path, which was ankle-deep in seawater now.

"Stand where you are!" someone shouted in a voice full of command, and at the sound of it Finn headed topside at a dead run, holding tightly to the parcel and the lamp. He heard the sound of running feet behind him, and he flung the lamp back down the path at his pursuer, where it shattered, a pool of oil flaring up as Finn ran on into the darkness, very soon seeing the dim light through the open hatch ahead.

He threw himself up the stairs into the storage room, grabbed the edge of the hatch, and slammed it down, full in the face of the man coming up, seeing him clearly and being seen in return. The hatch banged upward when the man's shoulder struck it, and then instantly down again, Finn's weight upon it as he yanked the bar into its hold-downs and slipped the latch into the iron bolt.

He stepped through the door into the kitchen and fixed the bolt on that door also, although it was long odds that the man would be able to open the hatch to follow him. They had come to take out the coffins before the sea did it for them, and they had no time to lose. Even so, it seemed to Finn that the woods were the safest bet for hiding, in case they came around to the beach to murder him. Out he went into the dusk, sliding the vellum package into his shirt as he ascended the chalk, not slowing until he reached the top and the handy perch on the cliff, the woods dark with shadows behind him now, the wind blowing through the sycamores.

The sun had disappeared and the rain was coming down now. His jacket, a grego left over from his oystering days, shed rain like ducks' feathers, and he held the hood low over his forehead with his left hand, thankful that it had been far too large for him when he'd bought it from a man in Billingsgate Market when he was… twelve years old? A lifetime ago, it seemed to him now.

In the deepening dusk he could see the white surf washing across the beach, the burnt remains of the paintings already swept away. Quicker than he would have thought possible the launch appeared on the heaving ocean, having rowed clear of

the cave. A wave rolled toward it, leapt up when it crossed a reef, and broke across the bay in a long wall, throwing over with a thunderous crash. The men waited for the whitewater to pass under the launch, and then in the moment of calm that followed they made a dash toward the open ocean, leaning on the oars, six straining silhouettes in the descending night. Finn could see the dark bulk of the coffins piled down the center of the launch, and he watched as the boat was very nearly thrown backward as it shot over the crest of the next wave.

The unbroken swells that followed lifted the launch skyward and then let it fall again, the men at the oars sprinting into the comparative safety of deeper water. The shifting lights of the steamship and its plume of smoke were still visible offshore where it rode at anchor. Despite the cold rain and the wind blowing hard across the cliffs, Finn stayed where he was, lingering for another half hour or so, watching the lightning flicker behind the clouds on the horizon. Finally the ship slanted away over the sea, its lights disappearing into the greater darkness. It was evidently moving north, looking for nearby shelter rather than south toward the Channel, which could be mortal in a storm.

The dark ocean swarmed up the beach now, the sea cave drowned. He stood up, realizing that he was famished as well as cold and wet. He thought of the meat pie and pudding waiting for him in a basket in the kitchen and the dry wood piled by the hearth. But food and a fire, he told himself, would be all the more welcome for the waiting, and he set out through the woods in the direction of Broadstairs.

CHAPTER Nine

THE SKELETON
IN THE CLOSET

Through the east-facing window of their room in the Albion Hotel the night was illuminated by flashes of lightning, the trees standing out starkly against the sky for a split second, their branches waving wildly in the sea wind, and then darkness again and the long boom of thunder. When the thunder died away there was the sound of rain and of surf beating against the cliffs and of the wind whistling under the eaves. The only light within their room was that of the log fire in the hearth, which was burning merrily, a pyramid of logs awaiting their fate in the rack alongside.

"I do love a storm," Alice said when the most recent grumble of thunder had passed away, "but I'm unhappy to think of Finn walking back to *Seaward* in it alone and at night, especially after that ghastly business in the sea cave."

"He relishes the walk," Langdon said. "I can't recall how old I was when a storm became less an adventure and more

of an inconvenience, but somehow it came to pass. Fortunately it's a short jaunt to *Seaward*. He'll be home by now, in fact, wearing dry clothes and with a fire lit. There's no sense in worrying about him. He is entirely persuaded that the smugglers completed their enterprise and sailed away."

"Peculiar smugglers. What use has anyone for dead men?"

"Students of anatomy find a use for them. There's a never-ending market for bodies. I recall them costing a week's wages when I studied anatomy at Edinburgh, but if several students went in snacks and cut the body up together, it was cheap indeed, and there was perhaps more to learn if your fellows knew what they were about."

"Went in *snacks!* What a terrible phrase. Did you often go in snacks?"

"I was never much of an anatomist," he said, shaking his head to underscore his statement, as if perhaps she wouldn't altogether believe him. "I prefer a living creature to a dead one, human creatures included, and I had no idea of doctoring as a career. But to answer your question about corpses, there was precious little profit in them, certainly not enough to account for the launch full of men and for the ship lying offshore. Finn did mention one curious thing, although it makes almost no sense and is a grisly subject. It'll make your flesh creep."

"I'm sure I can bear it," Alice said. "If I hadn't been in my pyjamas I'd have come down to the lobby myself. I want a full report. And in any event, the thing itself brings my uncle to mind."

"All right then, Finn tells me that he heard a movement within one of the coffins, and that he forced it open. In short,

he fears that the corpse was not quite dead. It was gibbering and gasping, apparently."

"Was it now? Did it gibber anything notable?"

"Not according to Finn. It was quite likely latent air escaping from the lungs or some other muscular spasm. The smugglers retrieved the coffins and so put an end to the mystery, practically speaking, and by now the tide has washed the cave clean. Why do you say that it brought your uncle into your mind?"

"I told you that he fell out of favor with the family."

"A skeleton in the closet, you said. Did the skeleton gibber?"

"We were compelled to tie its jaws shut with twine to silence him. He was a metaphoric skeleton, for the most part. I overheard my mother and father speaking of him, however. I was snooping, which puts me in a bad light. I regret to say that I had a habit of listening in."

"You should regret your regret, I say. What did you overhear?"

"Something to do with offensive books."

"*Lewd* books, do you mean? Salacious books?"

"No, something worse. I couldn't quite follow the whispering. Vellum illustrations made from the skin of corpses or something of that nature. Photographs of the dead. Magic lanterns to illuminate the pages and bring out the details. The victims' families were coerced to pay for the things, which led to my uncle's downfall. He was taken up by the police along with two cohorts, and charged with a variety of extortion. The lot of them were fined, but they avoided being hanged."

"These books, or something like them, might have accounted for the locked rooms that you mentioned."

"Assuredly, and for cousin Collier's being beaten, and perhaps later for his being driven from the house. In any event, there was a scandal when Uncle Godfrey was arrested, as you can imagine, but wealthy men were involved, and the details were pointedly obscure."

In the silence that followed, Alice listened to the rain, which ran down the window glass in sheets. The fire had burned to embers, and she thought of putting on another log, but she heard the sound of Langdon's even breathing and closed her eyes instead.

CHAPTER Ten

THAT DARK ROAD

ollier Bonnet sat alone in the Sparrow Tavern looking out at the rain that was slanting in off the sea in heavy gusts. The Cold Harbour steps had become a cataract, and a growing stream along the road carried a variety of filth toward the ocean. When the wind diminished for a moment or two, the misty air through the partly open window smelled of rotten sea wrack and dead fish.

Bonnet was waiting anxiously for the arrival of Alice, who, he had begun to believe, might never arrive at all—not merely because of the storm, but because she might have abandoned him to his well-deserved fate. He wouldn't blame her. He would abandon himself altogether if he had the gumption to tie the noose around his neck, climb onto the stool, and kick it over. But gumption was one of the several things he lacked.

Thinking of how low he had fallen, he heaved a sigh, which caught in his throat, an inch away from turning into

a sob. A glass of small beer sat in front of him, half drunk, and he looked down at it now with disfavor. It tasted of bread and was thick with sediment, but his father had taught him when he was a boy that two glasses of it passed well enough as breakfast, being real food and not mere fizz. His father, a drunkard but a naturally friendly man, had died years ago, and Collier, who had been sent to live with his uncle, missed what he remembered of his father, especially on lonely and desperate occasions.

He looked out for Alice again, and saw that a man had taken shelter beneath the overhanging second floor of a falling-down building across the way, the front façade having collapsed. A crowd of gulls clustered behind him, their backs to the wind. He was nautical looking, not apparently a vagrant, and he glanced now at Bonnet's window and then away again. He lit a pipe and settled in, the sea wind whirling the smoke away.

Bonnet's current hotel, the Latham, sat a mere fifty yards away at the foot of Paradise Street. The old cliff-side hotel let rooms by the hour, the day, the week, or the month, depending on the business that brought one to its dank neighborhood. Because of his temporary poverty, Bonnet slept in his caravan, or, on warm nights, in the mews with his ponies, his caravan out of view from the street. He washed himself at the pump, feeling moderately safe from his enemies, although that couldn't last. The hotel itself was a warren of rooms into which he could vanish with a moment's head start if his enemies found him.

There was some chance that Alice would *not* abandon him, of course. Not if she was the same Alice he had known these many years past and if time had not hardened her heart.

The leasing of *Seaward*, of course, might have turned the tide against him.

Bonnet picked up an old copy of *The American Review*, which sat beside his beer glass, open upside-down to "The Facts of M. Valdemar's Case," a strange story by Edgar Allen Poe about the horrors of the living dead, which he was re-reading. He closed the book, however, unable to attend to it.

He had come to believe that "The Facts of M. Valdemar's Case," which had been published with various titles over the years, was a story that was essentially true in its main details: a factual account as the title alleged and not a work of the imagination. Poe had been found delirious in the streets of Baltimore, very near death, dressed in clothes that were not his own and uttering the name "Reynolds" before dying of sheer terror—or so said the doctor who scrutinized Poe's face in the morgue.

The obscure Reynolds was in fact one of Poe's friends, unfortunately insane and a devotee of Franz Mesmer, the disciple of animal magnetism. To Bonnet's way of thinking, insane people told the truth as often as did people who were sane, perhaps more often, since lunatics generally said what they believed to be true, whereas sane people were often given to lying.

Bonnet wondered idly who the man across the way might actually be—a down-at-heels sailor sheltering from the storm, or someone more sinister. The rear door of The Sparrow was unlocked—he had made sure of it earlier, and he knew Esmeralda the bar mistress well enough to trust her. It was quite possible that she was sweet on him… He turned and caught her eye, and she gave him a wink and brought him another glass of beer.

"Waiting on a friend?" she asked, pushing her hair out of her face and putting a hand on his shoulder.

"My cousin Alice," he said. "I haven't seen her in…" He shook his head. "In many years."

"She's a right good friend if she shows up on such a morning as this."

"That she is—a *right* good friend." Unless, of course, she had given him up as a bad penny. Esmeralda patted his shoulder and went back about her business, leaving him to think.

In London some years back Bonnet had met Reynolds's son, who had taken up his father's profession and went by the name Baron Truelove. The Baron was interested in buying arcane books from him—autobiographical books, for lack of a more accurate word—books that Bonnet had stolen from his uncle, who badly deserved to be stolen from. Of necessity, each came with its own small Argand reading lamp, with a quart of lamp oil pressed from the corpse of the person whose life was the subject of the book. The pages could be read only until the oil was consumed, for without the lamp and the oil there was little to be seen on the pages.

They were horrible books—abominations—which Bonnet had looked into only on one occasion, in order to see for himself just what they were. Their value was breathtaking, however, if one found the right collector: enough to keep him in funds for the rest of his natural life. Or to end his life if he tried to sell them to the wrong man. Three days ago he had sent the Baron a note, naming a sum and asking that a reply be left at the Sparrow. Esmeralda had given him the Baron's reply this morning: "I'll find you," was all it said.

THE GOBBLIN' SOCIETY

Once again he considered the dangers of dealing with the Baron, death being uppermost on the list, especially given the enormous value of the books. But stealing the books from his uncle had cost him his inheritance, and selling the books would go some distance toward recouping it. *Take a long spoon when you sup with the devil*, he told himself, and in that moment he heard the creak of a door open behind him, and he half rose from the table, turning around to see who it was.

The man who called himself Southerleigh, President of the Gobblin' Society and wearing his pince-nez on a golden chain, opened his arms and said, "As I live and breathe!—Mr. Collier Bonnet himself, purveyor of fine books!"

CHAPTER Eleven

....

BREAKFAST

The dining-room at the Albion Hotel was bustling when St. Ives descended the stairs carrying the packet that Finn had given him last night. He had slept well, awakening to find that Alice had already gone out. He saw now that Tubby and Gilbert had secured a table and were sharing a pot of coffee and a rack of toast. Neither of them appeared to be happy, and Gilbert regarded his nephew with something like disdain.

The air was full of the smell of bacon, however, and at the next table a waiter was lifting the dome from a tray containing a broiled beefsteak, which seemed to St. Ives to be eminently necessary on this wet and windy morning, and there was nothing he could do about Gilbert and Tubby's never-ending wrangling.

He ordered beefsteak and eggs and filled his cup with coffee. "Cheers!" he said, holding up his cup, and his two companions did the same, although grudgingly. To distract them, he set the vellum packet on the table and opened it to

reveal the documents. From the corner of his eye, however, he saw someone gesturing from a nearby table. It was a man with a gaudy scarlet cravat who nodded to him in a familiar manner. St. Ives nodded back, thinking that he must know the man, who was now standing up out of his chair. St. Ives swept the packet under the table and out of sight.

"Perhaps you do not remember me, Professor," the man said to him, "but I recognized you as soon as you walked into the room. My name is Paddington, John Paddington. We met briefly at the Explorer's Club on the night that Bentley spoke about his discoveries along the Nile."

"Of course," St. Ives said, returning the man's smile, although he did not at all recall his face, let alone his name. "Allow me to introduce you to my friends: Tubby Frobisher and his uncle, Gilbert Frobisher. Tubby himself is a member of the Explorers Club these past fifteen years, and Gilbert is a great friend and patron to the Natural History Museum in Kensington."

"I associate your name with birds, sir." Paddington said to Gilbert. "You are largely responsible for the avian collection at the museum, if I'm not mistaken—a fabulous array of birds. I've spent a deal of time there."

"You are far from mistaken, Mr. Paddington," Gilbert said, smiling openly now. "I am that very man. Pray be seated. I'm happy to meet a fellow birder. Where do your interests lie—what sorts of birds?"

"All of them," he said, settling in at the table. "Anything that flies. I'm not particular. I don't want to impose upon you gentlemen for more than a moment. I have eaten, but I drink tea

after a meal to help with the digestion. I'll have the waiter fetch me a pot if you can tolerate my company."

St. Ives wasn't certain that he found the man's company tolerable, but Mr. Paddington was already calling for his pot of tea.

"What brings you to Broadstairs, gentlemen?" Paddington asked.

"We're here on holiday," St. Ives told him, "although the storm has us housebound this morning."

"These summer storms blow themselves out quickly," Paddington said. "A lot of sound and fury, and then the sun returns. They play the very devil with shipping, of course."

"Do you get to the Explorers Club often?" Tubby asked him.

"Not often enough, I'm afraid," Paddington said. "My usual club is Whites when I'm in London."

"Is it?" Gilbert asked. "I've been a member of Whites these many years. Where are you when you're not in London?"

"St. Leonard's. I've spent my life there, man and boy, and my father before me. I work for Clewe's, the great accounting firm, as did my father."

"And here you are in Broadstairs," Tubby said to him. "Holiday for you also?" He spooned strawberry preserves onto a triangle of toast and engulfed it in a single bite.

"I wish it were. I don't like to speak of it, but I was to meet my Canterbury cousin, Julian Hobbes, at this very hotel, but I have waited in vain. We intended to look into a family matter together, a rather sordid matter, alas, but it seems he has gone missing."

"Literally, do you mean?" St. Ives asked. "Perhaps he was merely detained in Canterbury."

"No, sir. Missing, I believe. I made inquiries and discovered that he arrived by coach in Margate and in fact made his way here to Broadstairs, where he simply vanished. I paid a boy to go round to the hotels in order to ask after him—a penny a hotel if he got the hotel stamp or a signature on a sheet of paper. He was a thorough lad and earned three shillings with a half-crown tip. If my cousin is lodged in Broadstairs it is at a private house and not a hotel. Last night I wired Canterbury to see whether he had perhaps gone home again, but he had not. That caused a dither in the household, as you might imagine."

"You referred to it as a sordid matter," St. Ives said. "Do you believe that he met with foul play?"

"I fear it, yes, although there's no evidence of it. Nor was he forthcoming with information except that he had an appointment with a man he referred to as the Baron. And that is the extent of my knowledge."

"The damned *Baron* again," said Tubby.

"You know of him, then?" asked Paddington, looking surprised.

"Of him, yes," St. Ives said, "given that he's the same baron. We certainly have no desire to know him any better. Unfortunately we haven't any idea where he's gone."

"And there were no other clues regarding your cousin's whereabouts?" Gilbert asked, looking keenly at him. "No useful address? A street name?"

"Only that a beggar claimed to have seen him turning up a lane that led to an old house on a prominence above Dickens Cove there along the Cliff Road—a 'culinary establishment,' the man said, specializing in game. It had a whimsical name—The

THE GOBBLIN' SOCIETY

Gobblin' Society, or so the man told me. He made eating gestures, and so I assume that he wasn't referring to hobgoblins or bogeymen, but was using the term in the American sense— short for 'gobbling,' do you see, very whimsical. The lane winds uphill to a gated property where it becomes a private carriage drive. I found the gate closed and locked, and I hallooed at the house for a time but got no response. I admit that it was early for an eating establishment to be open for business."

"You offered this beggar a reward before you posed the salient question?" Gilbert asked.

"I'm afraid I did. I take your meaning entirely: he might have given me false information simply to gain a shilling. I was struck by the term 'culinary establishment,' however, which seems too particular to be invented. Still and all, it came to nothing. There was no sort of sign on the gate, either, although the house sits alone on its prominence, and so there was no mistaking it."

"Perhaps it's a private club," St. Ives said.

The food arrived, platters of eggs and bacon, racks of fresh toast, and St. Ives's beefsteak. Mr. Paddington drained his cup. "I'll allow you gentlemen to eat in peace," he said. "I half think I'll return to St. Lawrence and leave the matter to the police." With that he stood up from his chair, nodded, and went off. A few moments later he could be seen through the window, hurrying beneath an umbrella to a waiting brougham, climbing in, and setting out through the falling rain.

"Strange that our Mr. Paddington hails from St. Leonard's but is returning to St. Lawrence," Gilbert said, hacking an egg

to pieces and mopping up the yolk with toast. "Did the two of you mark that?"

"Yes," said St. Ives. "A slip of the tongue, perhaps."

Gilbert shrugged, his eyes squinted. "Some variety of slip. I don't recognize the man from Whites."

"You're a behemoth of suspicion, Uncle," Tubby told him. "Allow me to remind you that you don't often get into London. You look into Whites once or twice a year. You and I have spoken of this—your habit of inventing sinister motivations for innocent strangers instead of seizing upon something valid."

"Valid be damned. I noted that his amber stickpin is a fake. The bee inside is far too well preserved, and the amber has a false cast to it. Fakery is no doubt a part of the man's makeup."

Tubby regarded him for a moment before saying, "The man knew that you had to do with birds, which recommends him. He knew you by reputation, which is an unvarnished compliment."

"Anyone who wants to know such a thing in order to perpetuate a fraud can discover it easily enough," Gilbert said. "His answer to my question was ludicrous. 'Anything that flies,' he said. I should have asked him about the red-necked phalarope. They're seen hereabouts, you know, a frightfully uncommon bird. The phalarope would have defeated him. And I've done business with Clewes. I've never heard of a Paddington at Clewes."

"Phalaropes, indeed. You regularly harbor suspicions of men you've never heard of, which is my point exactly."

"I *do*, by God, when there's reason to do it. Did you mark that he was loath to speak of his 'sordid' family business, and

then spoke of nothing else? You're a born contrarian, Tubby, anxious to prove your poor old uncle wrong."

"I'll remind you of the comely Miss Bracken, who very nearly fleeced you out of your money, and…"

Gilbert rose from his chair and walked out of the dining room, evidently in a state. In three minutes he returned, sat down, and said, "For your information, Tubby, the alleged John Paddington is not a guest at the hotel, nor had the hotel heard of any Julian Hobbes. So Paddington did not stay here last night or the two nights before that, which gives the lie to his claim that he has waited here for his cousin's arrival. He merely waited through breakfast in order to speak to us."

Tubby heaved a great sigh. "I apologize for dredging up the subject of Miss Bracken, Uncle, but to be fair to the man, who I find to be a dreadful bore, his stickpin included, I'll remind you that he did not claim that he or his lost cousin *stayed* in this hotel. They agreed to *meet* each other here. No end of people *meet* each other here. When you take the long view of it, everyone who does not sit alone in this dining room has *met* someone here. What did the man hope to gain by deceiving us?"

"A pot of tea, perhaps," St. Ives said, smiling at the two of them. "I've got something interesting to show you, something that might easily come to nothing." And with that he drew out the vellum parcel from beneath the table and related Finn's adventure in the sea cave and his own adventure this morning, in which he had found no caskets but had found the wooden litter of what Finn had described as a bench with no top on it. "Of course it was the Baron's hand again, these boxes or coffins. His lingering at *Seaward*

implies it. But I see nothing in this brief, coded manifest that casts a light on the affair. And here we have an alleged catalogue, as you can see, which seems to be little more than a list of names, at least at a hasty glance. I haven't given it a good look yet."

Gilbert picked up the single vellum sheet of the catalogue and scanned the columns of names on the first page, many of which names had a line drawn through them. "Here's Greenwood-Wright's name, by golly."

"And this name is meaningful to you, Uncle?" Tubby asked. "Do you have sinister suspicions of the man?"

"Pipe down, Tubby. Greenwood-Wright was an old friend, nothing sinister about him. We called him Lumpy at school, because he was prone to boils. He was quite an inventor in his day, especially in the realm of synthesizing gemstones. He sold his patent for their use in chronometers. I heard just a few weeks ago that he was at death's door. I meant to attend his funeral, but received no notice of it."

"My apologies, Uncle," Tubby said, taking the manifest and catalogue from him. He turned the catalogue page over, apparently reading every name. His eyes widened and he glanced up. "Here's a strange thing," he said simply, and he handed the catalogue to St. Ives, marking the place with his thumb. "Can this be explained?"

The word "Pending" divided the final column near the bottom. Above the word was written the name "Julian Hobbes, (head)" and below it were three names, the first two of which St. Ives did not recognize. The third name was "Langdon St. Ives."

CHAPTER Twelve

THE TRIAL

At the sight of Southerleigh entering the room, Bonnet leapt across to the front door and threw it open, wind and rain in his face. He thanked God Alice hadn't come, but the thought was barely formed when the nautical man from across the way loomed up, slammed him back into the tavern, spun him around, put his forearm around Bonnet's neck, and twisted his right arm behind his back.

Southerleigh bowed obsequiously and said that it was capital to see him again. Then he peered through his pince-nez at the cover of the book on the table, and said, "Ah, of course!" He plucked it up and the four of them went back through the rear door and into the office, such as it was—a round table with several chairs.

The farther door was padlocked, Bonnet's escape cut off. He was pushed down into one of the chairs, Southerleigh sitting across from him and Jensen taking up a position

behind, and the sailor standing by the door now. "I see that the ship is safely moored in the harbour, Mr. Baxter," Southerleigh said to the sailor. "When can you weigh anchor?"

"This afternoon, with the tide. The storm is blown out."

"The cargo is safely stowed, I take it?"

"Aye, safe enough. There was a boy in the cave last night having a look at it, though. He took the docket and ran."

"A boy? And he escaped you? The packet is lost, catalogue and all?"

"Bennett gave chase, but the boy scarpered. He was in through the hatch and slammed it shut, and that was that. It weren't for want of trying. The purser has copied out new papers, so there's nothing lost."

"Nothing lost, do you say? Secrecy is lost. You didn't think to go round to the beach in order to fetch him out of the house?"

"Aye, we thought of it, but there would have been no getting off the beach again, not through that surf."

Southerleigh was silent for a long moment. "Perhaps it played out well enough," he said at last. "Will play out, I should say."

He fell silent again, nodded his head as if satisfied, and said, "Go along back to the ship, Mr. Baxter. Tell Captain Feeney that he is not to risk the cargo, but that it is equally vital that he does not miss his tide. I will be along in a short while to speak to him on another matter."

"Well, sir," Southerleigh said to Bonnet, when Baxter had gone out, "we've been searching for you, hither and yon. I am quite worn out with it. Your traveling library had disappeared from the streets of Cliftonville. We were very much afraid that

you had fled, and now we are happy to discover that you have not. You must be right fond of Margate. Are you?"

Bonnet looked down at the table. "No," he said unhappily.

"Pull his ear, Mr. Jensen! Heigh-ho!" Southerleigh shouted.

Jensen gave Bonnet's ear an almighty twist, yanked it back and forth, released it, and then slapped it with his open palm. Bonnet cried out at the pain and at the suddenness of it, and he put his own hand up, feeling a warm line of blood trickling down his cheek. He breathed heavily and focused on steadying himself, on getting through this without being sick, although there was little in his stomach aside from beer. Southerleigh gazed at him with a wide-eyed cheerfulness, looking like a born devil.

"Well, this *is* an opportune moment, isn't it, Mr. Bonnet?" he said. "A crossing of paths, to be sure. Our luck is in—yours and mine together. You, of course, will do your part. Luck always favors them that does their parts, or so we're told. You believe the same, don't you, Mr. Bonnet—in doing one's part?"

"What I believe makes no difference whatsoever to you, Mr...."

"*Twist* his nose, Jensen!" Southerleigh shouted, and although Bonnet ducked his head, Jensen pulled him up by the collar, grasped his nose between two fingers and yanked it right and left, snapping his hand away to avoid the flow of blood from Bonnet's nostrils.

"*Mind your shirt-front, sir!*" Southerleigh said to Bonnet, looking dismayed. "Lean forward. That's it. Let it spill onto the tabletop. Jensen, fetch a damp rag from Esmeralda. Poor Mr. Bonnet's nose has seen fit to pour blood."

Jensen returned with a filthy rag that reeked of old beer, and Bonnet mopped his lip and chin and made an effort to staunch the bleeding.

"I'll tell you with all candor, Mr. Bonnet, what you most emphatically *do not* want to come to pass. You do not want Jensen to *gouge your eye.* He seems tolerably ready to do so. His thumbs twitch in anticipation. I appeal to you to respond to civil questions with civil answers. Is that agreeable to you or do you favor an eye-gouging?"

Bonnet nodded.

"Which?"

"Agreeable."

"*Quite* agreeable?"

"Yes, quite."

"Good. You meant to give this book to Alice St. Ives, did you not? You meant to call her attention to the story of M. Valdemar, thinking to betray the Society's little secret? Wait! Do not reply without consideration. And while you are considering, I'll ask a question of Mr. Jensen. Which eye is the simplest to pluck out?"

"The left eye, sir, me being a right-handed cove and standing behind as I am."

"Good. If I give you the word, remove Mr. Bonnet's left eye, but do not take the right eye, Mr. Jensen. A blind bookseller is of no earthly use to anyone. Do I make my meaning clear to you?"

"Very clear, sir."

"Eat the eyeball if you choose. An eyeball is a right succulent item, best eaten with salt and vinegar. And you, Mr. Bonnet, how do you answer the charge?"

"Yes," Bonnet said. "I fully intended to give Alice the book. It was an...ill thought out notion."

"I value your honesty, and I will be equally candid with you. The Society holds something of a grudge against you. You persuaded the Society to sign a yearly lease on your uncle's house without the legal right to do so. Mop your upper lip again, sir. I'm offended by the sight of blood. What do you say to this second charge against you—the problem of the fraudulent lease?"

"I deny it, with all due respect. I was asked to provide the lease, after all. I do not at all mean to contradict what you tell me, for I did in fact take one hundred pounds of the Society's money on three occasions, but I was compelled to do so, upon my word. The Baron..."

"You dither, Mr. Bonnet. You were entirely aware that the property was entangled in the probate courts, but you were not forthcoming with that information. You claimed it as your own. Do you dispute this?"

"No, sir. But you've had the use of the house and the sea cave these three years. I'll return the money, if that's what the Society desires."

"And how will you do that, sir? If you had the wherewithal to return the money you would not be sleeping in a horse stable. No, sir. We do not mean to ask for any recompense. We have another motive. In short, we have our eye on Professor St. Ives. His name has been added to the Catalogue."

Bonnet gaped at him. "What of Alice? You cannot ask that I betray my own cousin."

"We ask nothing of the sort, Mr. Bonnet. You know full well that the Society has no interest in women. We have strict dietary codes. I'll ask you to consider Article Fourteen, however, in the Charter. Do you recall it?"

"I know nothing of the Articles."

"I'll reveal it to you, then. 'If a willing visitor to a Society supper consumes human flesh he forthwith becomes a member of the Society, and so is forever subject to the Articles.'"

"I was not a willing visitor. My uncle compelled me, and he insisted that the meat was veal."

Southerleigh grinned at him. "Long pork would have been closer to the mark, but the savor of the human thigh *does* resemble that of a well turned out veal haunch. And yet once again you resort to the excuse of compulsion, which smacks of weakness. You are far too easily compelled. Imagine the fair Alice's horror when she discovers that her weak-willed cousin is actually a ravening cannibal."

"I deny it. I emptied my stomach into the shrubbery when I learned of the nature of the meat that I had consumed."

"Hah! What a fellow you are. I'm reminded of a gag I heard at Sadler's Wells. Infinitely droll, I assure you." He stared for a time at the ceiling and then bent forward, cocked his head, and said, "Have you heard tell, Mr. Bonnet, of the cannibal who passed his brother in the jungle?"

Without waiting for a response he laughed aloud, contorted his face, and bared his teeth in a comical grimace, exposing the sharpened incisors that made two pair with the eyeteeth. Abruptly the fit passed and he composed himself. "He was no

less a cannibal, do you see, despite the act of evacuation. That's the philosophical point."

"I repeat that I will not betray Alice," Bonnet said. "Gouge my eyes if you must." He sat up straight in his chair and looked Southerleigh full in the face.

"There's gumption for you, Jensen! For once in his life, Mr. Bonnet refuses to be compelled! He would rather have his eye plucked out. But we will prevail upon him to give us Professor St. Ives. Alice will be spared if he succeeds."

"And if I refuse?"

"Then I'll remind you that Article Seventeen insists that a member who betrays the interests of the Society will be consumed by the society. Put simply, you will watch through un-gouged eyes while we eat your cranial matter with sharpened spoons. You will be digested and summarily evacuated. Your fair cousin will be invited to witness the meal."

Bonnet stared at him, unable to speak. The door opened and Esmeralda looked in. "The woman's come in and gone out again like you said. She asked after him."

"Describe her for me, please."

"Nigh onto six feet tall, black hair, pert enough to turn heads. A thoroughbred. A likely looking boy was with her. Her name was Mrs. St. Ives, and she said I was to tell him"—she nodded at Bonnet—"that she was sorry to have missed him, the storm having made it necessary to change their conveyance. She's stopping at the greengrocer on Claymore Lane and then at the Crown Tavern, and after that up the hill to Cliftonville, to Clayton's Furnishings."

"She has gone away with the boy?"

"Yes, sir."

"Well done, Esmeralda. Fetch me a nib and inkbottle, if you will. And a sheet of foolscap, too."

She did as she was told, and then, before going out, she reached into her apron pocket and held her hand out to show Bonnet the three quid that she had clearly been paid to betray him.

"Now, Mr. Bonnet," Southerleigh said to him, "I am going to dictate a brief note to Professor St. Ives and you are going to write it out in a clear hand and place your signature at the bottom of it. If you refuse, I'll kill you where you sit and write out the note myself. The choice is yours." He placed the paper, pen, and ink in front of Bonnet and began to intone the message. When the task was completed, Southerleigh took the signed note, blotted it with another sheet of paper, folded it three times, and slipped it into the volume that contained the Poe story, marking the very page with it.

"Mr. Jensen," he said, "do me the service of going straight-away to the environs of the Royal Albion Hotel, Broadstairs. Find a boy to deliver this book to Professor St. Ives. Avoid being seen, of course. They would know you in an instant, and we would find ourselves dished. Do you understand me?"

"Aye, sir. *Now,* do you mean?"

"As fast as ever you can fly, Mr. Jensen."

Collier found himself alone in the room with Southerleigh, who drew a pocket pistol from his coat now and pointed it at him. "This is no time to cut a caper, Mr. Bonnet. You have very nearly won your freedom." He picked up the beer-and-blood-soaked

towel with his free hand and dabbed Bonnet's face in a motherly fashion, nodded in approval, and produced a wallet from his pocket. "Here is a ten pound note. For heaven's sake comport yourself like a man of parts so that the parts might continue to make up the man rather than a fricassee. You are to proceed to The Crown Tavern, there to rendezvous with Alice St. Ives. Send the boy away on some pretext. Dine with your fair cousin as you had promised to do. I adjure you to speak of inane things—pleasantries, happy times. Regale her with tales of your pitiful life as a bookseller. As you value the woman's happiness, say nothing of the note or the book that is even now hastening toward her husband.

"Remember, Mr. Bonnet, that the eyes of the Society are ever upon you, and upon your fair cousin."

CHAPTER Thirteen
....

GILBERT OUT ALONE

Wearing an oilcloth jacket against the heavy grey mist, Gilbert Frobisher walked alone along the Cliff Road, carrying his hazel wood walking stick. The Frobisher crest—a silver orb engraved with a rampant hedgehog, a flailing red devil in his teeth—was affixed to the top. The orb turned the stick into a springy weapon sufficient to crack a man's head open in the event that a man's head wanted cracking.

He had set out alone from the Albion Hotel, leaving Tubby and St. Ives to await Alice's return. Although he hadn't informed his companions, he had decided to put his morning constitutional to use by looking into the eating establishment that the man Paddington had mentioned, thereby looking a little more deeply into the man Paddington. If all was innocent then he would perhaps find something to eat.

He pictured confronting Tubby with a revelation about Paddington's tomfoolery. He loved his nephew, but Tubby

had the irritating habit of doubting him despite the authority that came with age, and it was a good thing now and then to take him down a peg. Tubby's assumption that the document from the sea cave somehow confirmed Paddington's innocence was simply another block-headed effort to have the last say.

Gilbert felt his earlier anger renewing itself, threatening to ruin the day for good and all, and he stopped to draw in a half dozen deep breaths, smelling the morning—a glorious amalgam of wet vegetation and sea fog. The sound of the breakers was muffled by the weather and by distance, the cliffs rising some three hundred feet along this section of coast. A line of eight pelicans rose above the cliffs now, dead even with Gilbert's head and flying northward, mere ghosts in the fog. He saluted them with his raised stick before they dipped out of sight.

"The only argument one wins," he told himself aloud, "is the argument one refuses to engage in." The sentiment restored him, and he went on his way, considering the possibility that Tubby was correct after all. The possibility of food activated both his mind and his stomach, and he rather hoped that Tubby *was* correct, and he wished that he hadn't left half his breakfast uneaten out of mere pique.

Gilbert was a charter member of the Marrowbone Club in Eastbourne, where he had eaten on many an evening over the course of the past forty years, and he intended to inquire into this Gobblin' Society despite its whimsical name. If it was sufficiently interesting—neither too elevated nor too facetious— then he would suggest a quid pro quo, perhaps combining the membership rolls to their mutual advantage. If he caught a whiff

of skullduggery, then he would look into it in his own way and bring his findings back with him to the hotel in order to fling them into Tubby's face.

He rounded a bend and saw a path winding downward toward the ocean just ahead, marked with a weather-beaten wooden sign on a post with the words "Dickens Cove" cut into the wood and picked out in black paint. On his left hand a lane wound upward between the trees, almost certainly the lane that led to the Gobblin' Society. A bench made of two wooden firkins and a plank was visible a short distance farther on along, probably the resting place of Paddington's beggar, although there was no sign of the man now.

Paddington's description of the area had been accurate, although it was unclear whether that made him more or less potentially sinister. Sinister men *did* exist, whatever Tubby might say to the contrary, and Gilbert had been shrewd enough in his time to see through a number of them, and to regret not seeing through others.

The mists swirled around him as he stood thinking. "I have it," he said aloud, and he fished his handkerchief out of his vest pocket. It too bore the Frobisher crest, and would be a beacon to anyone who knew him. He walked down to the signpost and tugged it firmly under a splinter of wood so that the handkerchief and its crest were visible, like a signal flag on a ship's mast.

He turned up the lane without hesitation now, feeling serious stirrings of hunger. As he rounded the curve in the carriage drive he saw the tall house, old and stately but rather morbid, its grey walls clothed in tall trees. Beyond an iron gate lay

wooded grounds, bordered by a high, stone wall. A pair of fat partridges stalked past beyond the wrought iron gate and disappeared again. Perhaps the establishment raised its own game, he thought, looking up at the lighted windows in the second floor, the glow of the lamps within diffused by the weather. It was a lonely place to be sure, but then everyplace was lonely on a day such as this.

He saw a bell now, hanging on an iron pole, and he strode up to it and gave it a shrewd clanging. After a few moments the door opened and a man with an abnormally round head looked out, saw him, waved heartily, and hurried toward him down the paved walkway.

"Greetings," he said cheerfully enough. "May I ask your name and your business?"

"Gilbert Frobisher at your service, sir. I've been told that this is in fact the home of a culinary society. I bring greetings from the Marrowbone Club in Eastbourne. Perhaps you've heard of us."

"Indeed I have!" the man said, sliding back the bolt that locked the gate. "Your chef has a luminous reputation. My name is Larsen, Harry Larsen. You've come up alone and on foot?"

"Indeed. I'm staying at the Royal Albion, where I was told of your establishment."

"Our good luck," he said, "and yours, too. It'll be thick as pea soup out here in another half an hour, and the coast walk is treacherous in a fog. We don't look for many members to drop in, not on a day like today, but coincidentally we have another surprise visitor and our chef is already cooking up something

to fend off starvation. Our man can take you back around to your hotel in the gig after you've sustained yourself with food and drink."

Gilbert cheerfully followed his host along the walk, in through the heavily carved front door, and into a vast room very like an inn parlor, illuminated by blazing gas-lamps and with a fire in the hearth. The walls were hung with heavy velvet curtains and tapestries, with here and there a nautical painting, and a wooden model of the derelict *Mary Celeste* on the mantelpiece. The mysterious ghost ship looked just as she was found, her sails ragged, her decks empty of people.

"May I take your coat, Mr. Frobisher?" Larsen asked him.

"You may, sir. And to come straight to the point of my mission, I would like to talk to you about the possibility of our two clubs forming an association, if your club is amenable to the idea."

"The board will be quite amenable, I'm certain," Larsen told him. "Shall I put your stick in the stand by the door?"

"I'll just retain the stick, I believe. I'm sometimes unsteady on my pegs."

"Of course. A glass of this capital amontillado, perhaps?" Larsen said, gesturing toward a heavily stuffed easy-chair near the fire. "Or would you prefer something more formidable? Brandy and champagne to whet the appetite, perhaps? That's the stuff on a day such as this."

"The sherry would suit me down to the ground," Gilbert said, sinking into the chair. "Brandy and champagne at this hour would put me to sleep. I'm not as young as I once was."

A door opened in the far wall, and a man walked in—a man wearing a scarlet cravat with an amber stickpin. "Mr. Paddington!" Gilbert said, taken aback to see him here.

"You two are acquainted, then?" Larsen asked. He handed the sherry glass to Gilbert, who tasted it and nodded with appreciation.

"Indeed we *are* acquainted," Paddington said. "We met a little over an hour ago at the Royal Albion Hotel. Mr. Frobisher and his friends were good enough to purchase a pot of tea on my behalf. I was in quite a taking, concerned unnecessarily about Julian."

"So you've found your cousin Hobbes, then," Gilbert said. "Your beggar was an honorable man after all?"

"He was, sir. When I left the three of you at the Albion I returned to this admirable manse. Mr. Larsen answered the bell, and I discovered that my cousin had overnighted on the property, and is leaving on the evening coach for Canterbury. It was all a simple confusion, do you see? Julian had left a message meant for me at the coaching station and the fool of a boy who took the message neglected to give it to me. That set the dominoes falling and resulted in my hurrying about like a madman."

Gilbert drank his sherry and nodded pleasurably at Larsen, who was smiling broadly at him. It occurred to Gilbert that the man wasn't entirely sober, but there was no call to throw stones. "What is that very excellent smell coming from the kitchen?" Gilbert asked. "Sweetbreads, perhaps?"

"Indeed," Larsen said. "Fried like oysters in flour and hot oil and sauced with malmsey. You'll take a bite to eat, Mr. Frobisher? We will set the table in this very room, if you gentlemen are inclined to

make a picnic of it here by the fire. The sweetbreads are a homely food, but very nice with blood pudding and toast points."

"I am fully persuaded of it," Gilbert said. "It would set me up wonderfully."

"I'll leave the bottle here on the table," Larsen said. "If it's to your taste, another bottle would go well with the sweetbreads. I must be off for a short while—business at the harbor. I expect the return of our President, Mr. Southerleigh, in due time. You'll like Southerleigh, Mr. Frobisher, and I'm certain he'll approve of this business of associating our two clubs. Do you have the leisure to wait for his return?"

"I'm rich with leisure," Gilbert said, seeing that the food was coming in now on a butler's trolley. He sipped his sherry and considered his rare good luck, which could only be improved if Tubby were with him.

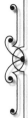

CHAPTER Fourteen

SHILLINGS AND PENNIES

Alice sat waiting at a table in the Crown Tavern, a cheerful place with a smoky fire. The tankard of bitter that she had ordered sat before Collier's chair. She drank hot cocoa, which was particularly good on such a morning, and looked out through the window. The blustery morning had led to a foggy afternoon. From her vantage point she watched Collier send Finn away. It made sense, since Collier would scarcely be frank with her if Finn was present, and it was still early enough for Finn to go along back to the Royal Albion and hence to Pegwell, the storm having blown itself out.

Collier walked back toward the tavern now, passing a man sitting beneath the portico, who plainly gave Collier a hard glance. Collier looked away, tripping on the threshold as he entered the tavern, and then slouched toward Alice.

"Well," he said, looking stricken and immediately drinking off half the tankard of ale, "here we are, Alice. Eh?"

"I daresay we are," she said. "You look frazzled, Cousin. Are you quite well?"

"As well as I deserve to be, no doubt. I'm sorry to have sent your boy away. He seems a decent sort. But I fear that our conversation might involve my…indiscretions…if you follow me." He drank again and cast her a feeble smile, and then looked out at the man beyond the window.

"Finn is happy enough to be sent away. He's anxious to be off to Pegwell to collect natterjack toads. Do you remember our passion for toads and frogs that one summer?"

"I do, alas. Does it ever occur to you that our happiest memories are also our saddest, for the mere fact that they're receding from us? Everything is obscured in time by the shadow of the gravestone."

Alice stopped herself from laughing out loud. "You still cultivate morbidity, Collier. My informant tells me that you've become the proprietor of a portable library. There's no hint of the gravestone in a portable library."

"Perhaps not," he said. "But who was your informant, pray tell?"

"A bird. Do you live hereabouts?"

"Hereabouts and thereabouts. You've come to take ownership of *Seaward*, then."

"Yes, I have. We're staying in Broadstairs tonight, however, at the Royal Albion. Uncle Godfrey's house needs a good airing and a general cheering up."

"The Royal Albion! Uncle took me there as a boy to dine in the big room. I ate most of a Strasburg pie. I doubt I'll ever taste foie gras again in life. I've become a gipsy, Alice. No fixed abode. I

quite prefer movement to being settled, and I've got *many* friends along the road. I lend them books and then collect them again. 'Pickwick's Portable Lending Library' at your service."

"Lending books for a *fee,* do you mean?"

"Oh, yes. The fee to the borrower is a shilling, and I return six pence when the book is given back. I buy the books second hand, from Mudie's, do you see—sixty volumes for five pounds. If a customer fails to return a volume, then he has paid a full shilling for it, which scarcely seems profitable, unless you remember that I've lent the book out any number of times before and so my initial investment is secure and I'm a shilling to the good. That shilling goes into a pot from which I pay to Mudie's for more books, buy food for the ponies, and treat myself to an occasional pint and beef pie."

"Shillings and pennies? It's no wonder you're thin as a rail. Do you need money?" She regretted her words immediately, which were too blunt and perhaps motivated by guilt, although very much to the point.

He shrugged and drained his glass. He was an overgrown boy, it seemed to Alice—the same Collier Bonnet she had known fifteen years ago, although somewhat more haggard and less likely to be amused. Certainly he had the same dramatic way about him, which made her impatient. The tap-boy appeared with plates of bangers and mash, and Alice said to him, "Bring another tankard of beer for the gentleman, if you will."

"I must not take advantage of your generosity," Collier said to her. "But I am persuaded that you asked your question out of a friendly candor, and so I'll respond in kind. I admit that I am low on funds." He broke off, his brave face collapsed, and he

began to weep. "You are *too* good, Alice, too frightfully good. I have come down in the world, alas, and have turned myself into a mere boat anchor, a bit of flotsam, a..."

"Nonsense," Alice said, heading him off. "One cannot be both a boat anchor and a piece of flotsam. The one sinks and the other swims."

His beer arrived, and he drank off two inches of it and then sighed heavily. "I'm afraid I'm of the sinking variety, or soon will be. I see that I must throw myself upon your mercy. Will you allow it?"

"Will I allow what, Collier? You're being obtuse."

"I'll reveal myself to you as frankly as I can, but you must not question me closely. It is not safe." He jerked his head toward the window at this juncture and lowered his voice: "The man you see sitting outside was sent to watch me. I'm out of favor with some bloody-minded men who form a secret society, cutthroats to the last man. I mean to disappear. I *must* disappear."

"You owe them a debt, these bloody-minded men?"

"In a word, yes."

"How much do you require?"

"Enough to get as far away as I can manage as soon as possible. I must leave tonight: by rail to Bristol and by ship to the continent."

"So you mean to flee rather than to pay your debt?"

"The word *debt* doesn't quite... In any event, once I've vanished, they will have no reason to cause either of us difficulties."

"Why would they cause *me* difficulties under any circumstances? Has this to do with Uncle Godfrey—something from the past that has come back around to threaten you?"

"Yes, after a fashion—something of my own making, however." He glanced at the window again and abruptly looked down at his plate, pushing it away. "Alas, my throat is closed. I am hungry and yet I cannot eat."

"Has this mystery to do with the coffins in the sea cave? The talking corpse?"

His head snapped up, his eyes wide. For a moment it appeared as if he would simply bolt. "*Yes,*" he said at last. "Is this your informative bird again? What else has it told you? Nothing, I very much hope. Already you know what you should not know, and yet you know only an incoherent fragment of the truth. Do not make light of this, Alice, for God's sake."

"I know nothing except that the sea cave is now empty, washed clean. Are they likely to return to it, these corpses?"

"Not at all likely. Your sudden appearance at *Seaward* set their plans awry."

"*Their* plans. Not the corpses' plans, surely? You must mean the plans of this cutthroat society. Who are they, these men? Can one reason with them?"

"No. They are in no sense of the word reasonable men."

"The despicable Baron, is he a member?"

"No, not entirely. He is something of a hireling, although a dangerous hireling. I find that you are mired more deeply in this business than is safe." He bent forward and whispered, "Do not mention the Baron aloud again, Alice, I beg of you. Have nothing to do with the man. If he speaks of me to you, *condemn* me. Throw me to the wolves if you must. And for God's sake, *forget what you think you know.*"

"Perhaps I will, but tell me, was Uncle Godfrey a member of this Society?"

He stared at her for a moment and then said, "Yes, although the Society had been around for many years before he signed the roll. Now, I have responded truthfully to the inquisition's questions, and I have nothing else to say about these men except that they would murder me if their secrets were revealed, and the murdering would not stop with me. To preserve the lot of us—to draw their gaze away from *Seaward* forever—it is necessary for me to vanish, as I said. No other outcome will do."

"I believe you," she said, "although I wish it weren't so."

He sat back in his chair, dusted his hands together, and looked out the window. "The storm is past, I believe. A sea fog often follows a summer storm hereabouts."

Alice stared at him for a long moment and then opened her purse and looked into it. "I have something over fifty pounds in bank notes. I give it to you happily as a gift, not as a loan." She drew the money out, folded the bills in half, and passed it to him beneath the table. "*Take it,*" she said when he hesitated, gaping at her like a deepwater fish.

He did as he was told, palming it neatly and slipping the money into his coat pocket. "I thank you with all my heart, dear Alice, but I must give you something in return. Is our man outside looking in at us?"

"No," Alice said after glancing at the window.

"Be so good as to hand me your muffler beneath the table."

She did so, and without taking his eyes off her face, he meddled with it, keeping it hid and handing it back to her as a heavy

package. She felt the hard outline of a pistol within its folds, and she quickly put it into her shoulder bag simply to get it out of sight. "I really have no need of…" she started to say, but Collier waved her silent.

"Reason not the need, Alice. You do not know enough to do so. I would be immensely happy to hear a week from now that you'd had no need of it. But if you do have need of it and do not have it, I would cut my throat myself before these demons had a chance to do it for me."

"Don't say such a thing."

"I've already said it, Alice. The gun is what is called a Peacemaker—short barrel pistol, once owned by our mutual uncle. It has six cartridges within it, and I have no others to give you. I've carried it these many years on my travels. You must keep it by you, although I'll warn you that it has a kick that can sprain your wrist. Have you shot a heavy pistol?"

"Many times, although only at inanimate things. I heartily dislike the idea of shooting at animate things unless I mean to eat the thing I shoot."

Bonnet swallowed hard and stared at her for a moment as if confused. "Yes," he said. "Of course. I mean to defend yourself or your family. You have no compunctions there?"

"No," she said.

"You relieve my mind. One last thing: the Society houses itself in the ole manse above Dickens Cove. You remember the place from our childhood?"

"What we called the haunted house? The high, shuttered house on the prominence?"

"Just so. Do not be lured to that house by any pretense, Alice. If, however, you find yourself there and are confronted by anyone you do not know, and I mean *anyone*, shoot him. He is guaranteed to be a monster. Promise me you'll do so."

"I feel as if I'm in a play, Collier. Are you being theatrical?"

"I would be a happy man if the world was a stage, Alice, but it is not. I'm deadly serious."

She nodded at him. "I'll do as you say, then, if it comes to it."

"I pray that it will not come to it. I must take my leave now. I do not begrudge you *Seaward*. I myself have made it impossible for me to live there. Tomorrow I will be either gone or dead. If things go well, I'll send a message by post from as far away as I can manage. Forgive me my sins against you, dear Alice. All of them."

He stood up now, and fishing in his trousers pocket he withdrew a creased bit of paper. "Do not read this, I pray you, until I am well gone." He began to say something more, but his voice hitched in his throat, and he merely shook his head sadly and went out. She watched as he set out across the road toward the adjacent park. The watcher beyond the window stood up and departed in another direction, and Alice sat alone at the table drinking cold cocoa.

After five minutes of waiting, she opened Collier's bit of paper, on which were scrawled the contradictory words, "If worst comes to worst, remember the haunted house, but do not go alone."

CHAPTER Fifteen

An Eye for an Eye

Finn stood behind the low sea-wall that swept in a curve around Margate Harbour. The heaving ocean was grey beyond the windswept rain, which came and went now as the storm clouds raced past overhead. Behind him stretched the Marine Parade, with its hotels and taverns, cheerful with lamplight. Few people were out and about on such a morning, and those that were hurried along, ducking into doorways or climbing into waiting coaches.

Alice's cousin Collier was an odd duck, sending Finn away from the Crown Tavern with a false and nervous smile on his face and an unnecessary two shillings as a bribe— unnecessary because Finn was already bound for the Albion to see about the Pegwell adventure and to report that Alice had elected to spend the balance of the day shopping. Finn had come by way of the harbour simply to see it, but what he saw had given him pause.

He watched a small steamship that lay at anchor at the far edge of sheltered water—the same ship that had been

anchored in the offing last night, with it's shed and crane. The launch that had taken the coffins out of the sea cave hung on davits at the stern. The Blue Peter flew from the ship's mast, meaning that the ship was ready to sail, no doubt waiting for the tide now that the storm was waning. The coffins almost certainly lay in the clipper's hold at this very moment.

A rowing boat with two men in it appeared from the seaward side of the steamship now. They wore oilskins, their faces obscured by mist, but as the boat drew nearer Finn was certain that the man at the oars was the very man who had pursued him in the sea cave. Finn had got a good look at him before he slammed the trap—the black beard and hard eyes. The boat angled in through the moored vessels, heading roughly toward Wardell's Hotel a short distance away to his left, where there was a stair from the beach up to the Marine Parade.

The man from the sea cave ran up onto the muddy shore now, and tied it to a ring bolt in the wall as the other man, very tall and thin, came on ahead of him toward the base of the stairs, his face shaded now by a broad-brimmed hat. Having no desire to be seen, Finn turned away and crossed the road, where he stood beneath an awning in front of a cigar divan, his own hat pulled low over his eyes. The man with the beard crossed to a gin shop and went in, and the other man walked toward Finn along the boardwalk.

Finn suppressed the desire to turn away, but he stayed put, wanting to get a good look at the man's face. He wore a pince-nez, which made his eyes look oddly close together. Not wanting to be obvious, Finn glanced away, and was taken aback when

the man stopped, looked hard at him, and asked, "What's your name, boy?"

"Lemuel Jones," Finn said. "They call me Lem, mostly."

"Were you watching the ship out yonder?" he asked, "and us rowing ashore?"

"Which ship, your honor?" Finn asked.

"The steamer. Don't lie to me. I saw your eyes upon us."

"If you saw such a thing, why do you ask?"

Without warning the man said, "Boo!" and attempted to strike Finn a backhanded blow, but Finn ducked under it and backed out of the way. The man laughed aloud and went into the cigar divan, shutting the door behind him.

Finn walked back toward the sea-wall, feeling the flush of anger and insult rising in his face. He had never been fond of either, and had long ago had his fill of mean-spirited men. He glanced back, saw no one watching him, and descended the stairs to the beach where he untied the rowing boat from its ring and pushed it out into the water, stepping into it and shipping the oars.

He was afloat in a trice, weaving through the moorings toward where several boats much like the one he sat in were serried along the wall, out of the wind and chop. He moved in among them, found a handy buoy, and tied up. The two men could whistle for their boat. He stepped over the gunwale into shallow water, drowning his already wet shoes, and saw that there was a piece of oiled sailcloth in the stern of the boat, shoved under a thwart. For good measure he pulled it out, stretched it across from stem to stern, and fixed it tight. Now the boat might be any boat at all. Perhaps they would never find it. It was no concern of his.

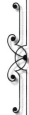

CHAPTER Sixteen

THE BARON'S BARGAIN

Bonnet walked across the park and into the warren of streets beyond, cursing himself for the mess he had made of things and the things that he had lost as a result—Alice for one of them. It came into his mind that he should repair to Broadstairs to reveal everything to St. Ives, except that Southerleigh would very soon know that he had done so, and lives would be forfeit. And yet it seemed cowardly to leave things as they stood. He had never been a hero. But how many men were heroes—or women for that matter? Alice, perhaps, he thought shamefully. But surely this was not cowardice on his part. He must finish his business with the Baron, if only he could make one last bargain before he disappeared. If he failed, and Alice's fifty pounds was all he had to travel on, so be it. He would know for good and all that he was born for poverty.

A wave of regret came over him for having signed Southerleigh's note. He should have attacked the villain

where he stood, taken his pistol away, shot him dead, and raced to the Crown Tavern to warn Alice. But he had not. Surely St. Ives was too wary to take the bait, what with his knowledge of the corpses in the sea cave. He had already met the Baron, for God's sake, had seen the face of evil first hand.

Should he have told Alice of the note...?

He dismissed the idea. It would simply have sent her to her doom. It was enough that she knew the truth about the old house. If St. Ives was taken, that would be his destination, since the Society meant either to eat him or to turn him into one of the living dead.

At this moment the Baron himself stepped out of the mouth of an alley, his face shaded by his broad-brimmed hat. The Crown Tavern was out of sight behind them, thank God.

"Might I have a word with you, Mr. Bonnet?" the Baron said, gripping him by the elbow. "I see that you have been dining with the St. Ives woman."

"Yes," Collier said. "I dine with whom I choose. I assured Southerleigh that I would be circumspect, and so I was. I was simply carrying out a duty that..."

"I care nothing for your circumspection, or your duties, or for Southerleigh's demands. I am not one of Southerleigh's minions, and it might surprise you to hear that I have no taste for human flesh. I would wish Southerleigh to Hell, but it would be superfluous. Now, sir, if you have the time, I would like to conclude that matter of business. Time is unfortunately short."

He stepped over a dead cat that lay in a pool of rainwater, stiff as a frying pan, and lead Collier into the comparative

darkness of the alley. "I'll speak plainly," the Baron said to him. "I am indeed interested in purchasing the two volumes that you purloined from your uncle."

"I *earned* them by my suffering, sir, and as you know my uncle is dead. I did *not* purloin them."

"I assure you that I am indifferent to your crimes and, alas, to your sufferings. I will purchase the volumes, as I say, but not for the sum you suggested. I tell you plainly that if you have other collectors interested in the books, you might look to them for an offer. Mine will not last out the evening, however, so you'd best hurry."

Collier stood thinking for a moment, watching the Baron's face. Of course there were no other offers, and the Baron knew it full well. It was time, it seemed to Collier, to seize fate by its forelock, an idea that sent a thrill of fear through him. "If your price is sensible we'll settle it here and now," he said.

"Good. I had been afraid that you would prove shy. We both feel the unease, so to put it, which emanates from the house on the hill. Our mutual friend the President is too facetious by half, as you know. I believe that he is mad, to put it simply, and poisoned by his filthy habits. His cohorts are unsteady and given to risks. The man Forbes is a drunkard, and Larsen is too often stupefied by opium. Chaos, Mr. Bonnet, is in the offing. I intend to flee before it, to leave without notice."

"That would suit me down to the ground, Baron. Make your offer," Bonnet made an effort to sound resolute. The man's bluff tone had a false ring to it: perhaps of treachery, perhaps of opportunity, most likely both.

"I'll tolerate the sum of two thousand pounds per volume, paid down in Bank of England notes."

"*Tolerate* it? The books are worth ten times that, as you are fully aware."

"I'm equally aware that there are men who will eat you and throw your bones into the sea if you do not make yourself scarce. *Four thousand pounds* for the two, Mr. Bonnet. It is enough to keep you in food, drink, and lodging for a very long time. That sum, to the penny, is available to me." He removed a watch from his breast pocket, looked at it, and put it away again, shaking his head. "I must be away before nightfall. If you are a sensible man, you will do something of the same thing, telling no one of your destination. The salient question has to do with which of us will carry a valise containing books and which will carry one containing banknotes."

"We've answered that question already," Bonnet heard himself say, his voice as bluff as he could make it. "I accept your terms. I suggest that we meet in a private place that we both know: the sea cave at Lazarus Bay, say in four hours' time. The St. Iveses and their friends are in Broadstairs. Only the boy is staying at *Seaward*. To the best of my knowledge he is bound for Pegwell for the afternoon and will be out of the way. I am certain you are aware of the hidden entrance to the cave through the rock cleft in Blakely Cove, just to the north. Even if I'm wrong about the boy, he knows nothing of the second entrance. We can conduct our business in the room beneath the floor of the old out-building. You'll no doubt want to light the corpse-oil lamp and see the effect on the pages, which is something that must be done in secret."

"Indeed I will, Mr. Bonnet. I have no idea of paying for counterfeits. The cave will serve, but mind you, I will be armed. I tell you that in case you mean to betray me."

"Or in case you mean to murder me," Bonnet said.

"There's no point in my doing so, I assure you. I am a man of business, and my sole interest is profit. There is no profit in being hanged."

CHAPTER Seventeen

LIVING DEATH

St. Ives and Tubby Frobisher sat in the lobby of the Royal Albion Hotel in the early afternoon quiet, having just read a note from Gilbert saying that he had set out on his midday jaunt and would return in time to make the trek to Pegwell if that were still on the calendar, which it very much was as soon as Finn arrived.

A boy came into the lobby now, accompanied by a dour faced doorman. The two stopped for a moment, and then the doorman pointed in St. Ives's direction, and they came on again. "I'm to deliver this here book," the boy said, "to a Mr. St. Ives."

"Capital," St. Ives said. "You've found him." He took the proffered book—a copy of *The American Review* magazine with a paper cover, rather than a proper book. A folded note protruded from between the pages, and he glanced at it long enough to see that it was signed by Collier Bonnet, of all the confounding things.

"The man give it to me out on the road with a tuppence, and off he went in a terrible hurry."

"Then here's a shilling to add to your tuppence," St. Ives said, handing over a coin, thinking that it was curious that Bonnet should have met with Alice in Margate this very morning, and so could simply have given her the note rather than coming into Broadstairs and having a boy deliver it. The doorman led the boy away, and St. Ives quickly read the note, Tubby looking on. "This is an odd business," he said.

"If there's nothing secretive in it," Tubby said, "pray read it aloud."

"*The smugglers' ship lies in the harbour at Margate and will sail today with the tide when there's depth enough to cross the bar. It is the* Zealous *steamer, 80 feet, out of Plymouth, bound for Calais and smuggling bodies. The story in this book tells the tale,* and your name is in their catalogue! *You can take them if you hurry and put paid to their caper. The harbour master, whose name is Plank, is no fool—he nor Constable Watley both. Meet them at the blue shed where the crane sits along the sea-wall for unloading, and the lot of you can round up the few men on board the* Zealous, *which the crew is bowsing up their jibs ashore presently and the ship will be undermanned if you hurry. A skeleton crew. Tell Plank who you are and you can take the ship together. I dare not be involved, nor must Alice. Your Servant, Collier Bonnet.*"

"*Bowsing up their jibs...*" Tubby said. "A *skeleton* crew smuggling *bodies?* Would Bonnet write a desperate letter in this frivolous manner? Either he's jesting or he's half mad."

"I've never spoken to him, so I cannot attest to his sanity, but Alice has described him as silly-minded and capricious, and you'll recall that his previous note, addressed to her, was pitched at her from the top of the cliff."

"Is it sensible that he would have knowledge of this so-called catalogue that Finn took out of the cave? Neither Finn nor Alice would have mentioned its existence, surely, let alone that your name is on the list."

"It is possible, yes. He's privy to secret elements of his uncle's life, and, of course, he was an associate of the Baron, although perhaps unwillingly."

"He risks being taken up by the police for illegally profiting from *Seaward*, and yet he lurks nearby amusing himself in this cryptic fashion. Bonnet must have something to gain, perhaps at your expense."

"Yes, but they've succeeded in drawing me in." St. Ives looked into the book, noting the story that was printed upon the page marked with the note. "Have you read Mr. Poe, Tubby?"

"Not unless he's still alive and writing for *The Sporting Times*. My interest in literature has a great deal to do with horse racing and not very much else. But I've heard of the man, sure."

"It's been some time since I've read this dismal story, but the essence has to do with the hypnotizing of a man at the point of death—*in articulo mortis*, if you will—with the intent of cheating death itself. The man would live on in a state of partial consciousness as his body declines."

"A living death? I don't believe it," Tubby said. "This is beginning to smell like a hoax."

"We must remember that our old friend Narbondo effected something of the same thing, employing the glandular secretions of carp. And a similar result was achieved by witch doctors on the island of Haiti, who poisoned victims with the organs of the porcupine fish, turning them into what are referred to as zombies in that part of the world. Who's to say that hypnosis cannot effect the same thing?"

"Not Tubby Frobisher, I assure you. And, as you've already pointed out, there's the interesting fact that your name appears in the catalogue."

"Yes. Will you accompany me to the harbour, Tubby, to see this man Plank?"

"As soon as I fetch my blackthorn cudgel. I don't much like any of this, least of all your man Bonnet's letter."

"We'll hire the Albion's cab to take us into Margate and leave a note for our friends, whoever returns first. We must not merely vanish like the man Hobbes and so become a part of the mystery."

In five minutes they were away, the fog swirling into their faces, the trees in the adjacent woods mere shadows near-to and invisible forty feet away. They could hear nothing from beyond the noisome world of the interior of the hansom—the clip-clopping of the horses' hooves and the talk of the driver through the open hatch above as he spoke to the horses, urging the pair along the road at an immoderately rapid pace. The horses knew the road, however, the mud and stones flying from their hooves and from the wheels, thudding against the fender. Soon they swerved around a bend and came out onto the Cliff Road, the sea visible off to the right.

"There's the signpost Paddington spoke of—Dickens Cove," Tubby said, pointing toward a rocky passage leading downward toward the beach.

"And there's the beggar's lane up the hill," St. Ives said, nodding in the other direction as they ran past it, although there was little to be seen but grey mists. Moments later they passed beneath the ghostly branches of Alice's yew tree, and in a short time they clattered past the North Foreland Light and onto the long curve around Foreness Point. Margate itself had to be taken on faith, shrouded as it was in fog.

FINN HAD IT IN his mind to run all the way into Broadstairs, but he hadn't quite reached Botany Bay when a hansom cab loomed up out of the mist and clattered toward him at a promiscuous speed. He leapt into the tall grass beside the road, not realizing until the cab had thundered past that the Professor and Tubby sat within. Although Finn shouted after it and waved his arms, the cab flew out of sight and sound.

His way was suddenly unclear to him. Two things would have drawn the Professor and Tubby into Margate in such a tearing hurry: a note from Alice or word of the steamship in the harbour. At The Crown Tavern, Collier Bonnet had been frightened of something, although to be sure it might have been Alice herself that he was frightened of. Something was afoot, that was certain, and he turned and headed back into Margate, running now. If he failed to find them at the harbour, he would make his way to Clayton's Furnishings in Cliftonville.

He oughtn't to have left Alice alone at all. He had been a fool not to have seen it before.

ST. IVES AND TUBBY climbed out of the cab at the bottom of King Street. They could scarcely see the harbour, and they stood for a moment taking their bearings. A land breeze blew in fits and starts, however, opening windows in the fog, one of which revealed the steamship, moored in deep water off the far end of the sea-wall, dark smoke rising from its stack.

The two of them set out around the wall, making out the crane and crane-house when they were nearly at its door. There was lantern light within, and through the window St. Ives could see three men playing cards at a round table. Tubby rapped on the door with his cudgel, and one of the men reached over to swing the casement open. "What's your business?" he asked.

"We're looking for the harbour master, a Mr. Plank. My name is Langdon St. Ives, and this is my friend Tubby Frobisher."

"Aye, I'm Plank," the man said, "and this is Constable Watley and his man Jones. You're here about the *Zealous* steamer, then. Mr. Bonnet told us something of it, although the man's account was a strange one. We'd best move along if we want to look into it. Most of the crew are ashore, but there seems to be some possibility of a dangerous reception, so sharp's the word."

Plank closed and latched the casement, and came out through the door. He was an abnormally thin, tall man with a pince-nez over his right eye and a toothy smile. His second incisors were uncommonly sharp, as if they had been filed, and it struck St. Ives

that the man looked too eccentric by half—more like a ghoul in a side-show than a harbour master. Constable Watley came along behind, as did Jones, a heavily muscled man with hairy arms that reached nearly to his knees. Plank led the way along the curved wall, the harbor wheeling away to the left. Small boats lay moored below them, most of them afloat now that the tide was at the turn.

"Let us talk as we walk," Plank said. "We were hoping that you could cast a light on Mr. Bonnet's story, which sounds unlikely. I'm not certain of the man's sanity."

"We haven't much light to cast, I'm afraid," St. Ives said. "We do know that several coffins were taken out of a sea cave at the south end of Lazarus Bay at dusk yesterday. The incident had all the earmarks of smuggling except that of evident profit. How Mr. Bonnet was aware of it I can't say, but we received this note from him not half an hour ago at the Royal Albion in Broadstairs. We set out directly."

St. Ives handed Plank the note, and the man read it. "I don't know Bonnet aside from his seeking me out this very morning in order to tell me his tale. Is he trustworthy?"

"He is my wife's cousin," St. Ives said. "I've never met him. She would say that he was trustworthy, within limits. He stands to gain nothing by deceiving us."

"He mentions a list. Do you know the meaning of the term?"

"Indeed. It seems to be a sort of catalogue of goods offered for sale by the smugglers. My name appears on it."

"Does it now? *Your name?* Do you mean to say that the names—the men whose names were on the list—were in some sense *for sale?* Something like a slaver's manifest?"

"My uncle recognized the name of a dead friend," Tubby put in. "A dead man would make an indifferent slave."

"It is a mystery without essential meaning," St. Ives said, "but that's the long and the short of it."

"And how did you come by it, this catalogue? Forgive me for this interrogation, but I wonder what we're walking into, if you follow me."

"My...adopted son was exploring the sea cave. These papers, wrapped tightly in vellum, were affixed to one of the coffins. He carried the packet out when he fled from the smugglers."

"I very much hope that you brought them with you, Professor," Constable Watley said, speaking to St. Ives's back. "As evidence, I mean to say."

"I did just that," said St. Ives, looking over his shoulder. Watley had an enormous head, which seemed to teeter on his neck like a pumpkin on a stalk. He handed the single page to the man, who scowled at it, shook his head, and tucked it into his coat.

They were at the end of the sea-wall now, the fog swirling in the breeze, thinning momentarily and then thickening again. The deck of the steamer was still apparently empty, although it seemed to St. Ives that there must necessarily be a fireman aboard to keep the oven supplied with coal and someone else to stand watch. Moored to a stone dock below them floated a long rowing boat with four seats and with oars in the locks.

Jones descended the stairs to the dock, stepped into the boat, and untied the bow rope from its bollard before taking his seat. "Climb in, then, mates," he said. "I'll hold it steady."

THE GOBBLIN' SOCIETY

"Be careful, gentlemen," Plank said. "I must return to my work. My complements to you gentlemen for doing your duty." He shook St. Ives by the hand, nodded to Tubby, made an abrupt about face, and set off up the several stairs and back along the sea-wall, disappearing into the mist. His leave-taking seemed as odd as the man himself, given his mentioning the possibility of a dangerous reception on the steamer only a few minutes past.

Constable Watley stepped into the boat and sat down in the stern. They were near the tip of the sea-wall, and an incoming wave lifted the boat, knocked it against the dock, and dropped it again. "Mind the surge," Watley said, and he took St. Ives's forearm and held on until he was situated, his back to Jones. Tubby stepped in heavily now, the boat tipping precariously under his weight. Jones shoved off hard as Tubby teetered backward, nearly falling atop Watley, who set his hands on Tubby's lower back and leaned into him. Tubby pitched forward now, waving his arms for balance. He held onto his blackthorn club with one hand and attempted to grapple the gunwale with his other, shouting for Jones to row steady, for God's sake. The boat passed into the fog, and another swell took them side on, the boat tilting sharply so that Tubby dropped his blackthorn in his effort to catch himself.

"I've got it!" Jones cried, and he shipped the oars wildly now, flinging water and knocking Tubby overboard.

St. Ives leant out to grab Tubby's coat, but a coil of rope dropped over his head and shoulders and was yanked tight from behind, his arms pinioned. Watley removed a pistol from his coat, pointed it at St. Ives, and shouted, "Steady-on!"

Tubby grabbed onto the gunwale and attempted to climb in, very nearly scuttling them, and Watley swung the pistol toward him and fired wildly, Tubby hurtling backward into the water, the boat pitching wildly. In that moment St. Ives was clubbed from behind and he fell into the bottom of the boat.

AS HE RAN OUT along the sea-wall Finn watched Tubby's strange antics in the pitching boat, and he nearly ran headlong into the grinning devil with the broad-brimmed hat and pince-nez who had confronted him on the Marine Parade not an hour ago—the chief of the smugglers, no doubt. The man was looking down toward the beach, thank God, and Finn slipped past unseen, wondering what he was doing there, why Tubby and the Professor were in the rowing boat with two strange men. It made no sense except bad sense.

He lost sight of them for a moment as he passed the crane house and the buildings alongside, and when the boat came into view again everything had changed. St. Ives was struggling with the man behind him, and Tubby was in the water, reaching for the gunwale. The man in the stern held a pistol, and he shot at Tubby now—a brief shower of sparks against the grey fog. Tubby disappeared into the water, St. Ives slumped forward, and the boat vanished from sight.

Shoving his spyglass into his coat, he ran back along the sea-wall to where he had left the stolen boat. He saw the back of the man with the pince-nez, nearly to the Marine Parade now, and good riddance. The tide was coming up fast, raising his boat

out of the muck, and it took but a moment for Finn to slog out to it, yank the canvas off and fling it away, untie the rope from its buoy, and push it clear of its neighbors. He swarmed over the side, fixed the oars, and rowed down a narrow lane into open water, looking out for Tubby, although there was little to see in the murk. He shouted Tubby's name, paused to listen, shouted it again, wheeling around in the direction of the ocean now, rowing slowly and shouting at intervals.

The land breeze gusted, and Finn saw Tubby swimming feebly, pushed shoreward by the making tide. He gripped his cudgel in his right hand, which hampered his swimming, but Finn was happy to see the he hadn't lost it. He wished he had a cudgel of his own. He caught up to him with two hard strokes, and then backed water to come alongside without knocking him on the head. He shipped the oars and leaned over the side precariously, trying to get a purchase on Tubby's coat. "You've been shot," he said, seeing the rill of blood running down from where the bullet had creased his scalp.

"It's nothing," Tubby gasped. "Thank God I fell when I did, or he'd have murdered me else. They've taken the Professor, Finn. I'll grab on astern while you row us ashore. There's something we must do to save him, but God knows what it is."

"Alice will know, if only we can catch her," Finn said, rowing hard, dragging Tubby along behind.

Tubby's feet found the bottom and he let go, Finn driving the boat onto the now-submerged beach where it grounded, and the two of them hauled it up and tied it to the iron ring. Tubby was breathing heavily, attempting to staunch the blood flowing

from the crease on his head with his wet kerchief. Finn took his arm and helped him up the several stairs, where they turned to look at the steamer, the sea wind momentarily having blown away the mists. It was steaming out toward the bar, its ship's bell clanging to warn other ships of its ghostly presence.

CHAPTER Eighteen

THE RISING TIDE

Collier Bonnet set his lantern on a shelf cut into the chalk in the sea cave and busied himself with preparations for his meeting with the Baron. He could hear the churning of the waves in the distance, and the air was cold and wet and smelt of rotting seaweed. Now and then a gust would whoosh through, followed by a painful pressure in Bonnet's injured ear, which meant that a breaker had slammed entirely across the cave mouth. His hands shook, he gasped now and then due to forgetting to breathe, and since leaving the Baron in the alley, his head had been full of bees. There were good odds that he would die in this wretched cave and be eaten by crabs, Alice finding his skeleton wedged into the rocks.

His copy of *The Nautical Almanac* predicted a high tide of nearly eight feet later this evening, and with the surf still running, the sea cave at *Seaward* would be inundated long before the tide peaked. He had no reason to believe that the Baron considered the tides.

It came into his mind that although the Baron would cheerfully commit murder, the man would avoid that extremity until he himself possessed the books or else believed that Bonnet meant to cheat him. Each of the two books was wrapped securely in several layers of oiled silk; the packages enclosed in decorated Christmas tins that had originally held biscuits. The tins were housed in leather-covered wooden boxes, their small lamps and pints of lamp oil reclined in padded niches of their own. The boxes lay within the darkness of the criss-crossed ceiling beams—the beams that supported the floor of the room above.

Near the hidden books was a coil of rope, old but serviceable. Bonnet hesitated to consider in what *way* it might be serviceable, since it had to do with murder. He wondered whether tying a man up in order to let him drown was as sinful as beating him to death and allowing the ocean to take his body out with the tide. In either event, an inert Baron could not murder him. And if he was *compelled* to deal decisively with the Baron, then it stood to reason that there was no further sin in taking the Baron's money away with him. What did a dead man want with money?

He bent over and gathered up a handful of fine dry sand and put the sand into his trousers pocket. Then he felt for the handle of the rusty hammer from the storage room. He had slipped it head-downward into the deep back pocket of his trousers, the top of the handle sticking up out of the pocket, easy to snatch if the time came. *When* the time came, for it would surely come. He must steel himself for it. Better a live murderer than a dead coward, he thought philosophically. He flipped his coat aside and snatched out the hammer, taking a swing at the empty air,

cutting down an imaginary Baron but very nearly hitting his own knee.

Taking up the lantern, he walked down through the cave as far as the wide cleft that led into the side-passage. The cleft was well hidden despite it's size. Unless one was a smuggler with secret knowledge, one would have to search for it, which, of course, one would not know to do. Various planes of rock overlaid each other there, and only by sidling past the first edge of rock into a dark and narrow stone cupboard, so to speak, could one see that there might be a way through. A leafy stand of trees and shrubs masked the far-away exit along the base of the cliff above Blakely Cove just to the north. The Baron would necessarily appear from this passage unless he, too, had retained his keys to *Seaward*. He turned to retrace his steps when there was again a heavy thump, another gust of wet wind following close on, and that followed by a surge of seawater that washed over his feet.

He wished again that the Baron would hurry himself along. In half an hour the cave would be flooded and it would be too late. In the space of a moment his wish was granted: the Baron *had* kept a key to *Seaward*, and had come in through the kitchen, and now the bar of light from the partly open hatch widened into a yellow rectangle on the sandy floor. He saw the Baron's feet and legs descend the stairs, and then he pulled the trap down behind him, the cave darkening by half. He carried a lantern, the twin of Bonnet's from the room above, and there were two little islands of light in the darkness now.

"Hello!" Bonnet said to him. "You've come, have you?" He realized that he sounded foolish—insincere, God save him.

"Indeed I have," said the Baron, walking forward and setting his own lantern onto the shelf where Bonnet's lantern had been. His other hand held a Gladstone bag. He squinted at Bonnet and cocked his head. "I'm troubled to see that you are empty handed, Mr. Bonnet."

"Not so empty as it might seem," Bonnet said, immediately regretting the stupidity of the phrase. He quelled the impulse to bolt down the passage.

"Mind yourself, my young friend," the Baron said. "Southerleigh has offered me a considerable sum to deliver you to him now that he has no use for you. The Society is hungry, or so he tells me. I regret to say that they'll have their pound of flesh if this falls out badly. Let us make the exchange simple and quick, eh? We'll let the cannibals sing for their supper."

"The books are nearby, Baron, safe as…doormice. Let me see into the bag."

"Of course. Count the money if you'd like. Then I'll have a look at the books. Fair is fair." He opened the Gladstone bag and held it out.

Bonnet put his free right hand into his pocket and walked forward, noting that the Baron's eye was upon him. He raised his own lantern as if he intended to illuminate the bag, but he had no idea of counting the money, only of narrowing the distance between them. He clutched as much sand as he could hold and forced himself to breathe evenly. It was death or glory now.

The Baron reached into his coat, drew out a revolver, and cocked it, and without a moment's hesitation Bonnet flung the sand straight into his eyes. The Baron reeled backward, dropping

the bag and pawing at his face with his forearm. Bonnet snatched out the hammer, leapt forward, and struck him a heavy blow on the side of the head. There was a hollow *thunk* and a spray of blood, and the Baron fell onto his side, the pistol firing randomly, incredibly loud in the confines of the cavern. The Baron screamed, the toe of his boot having burst apart. To Bonnet's amazement, the man had evidently shot himself.

The Baron grunted and rolled over onto his stomach, waving the pistol in Bonnet's direction now, blasting away twice, pieces of chalk flying, one of the fragments tearing a line in Bonnet's cheek. Desperate to hide from the light, Bonnet put his lantern down and leapt back down the passage into the darkness. From the shadows he could see the Baron on his knees now, bracing himself with one hand, the pistol ranging back and forth. His face was a mixture of pain and loathing.

There was an ear-throbbing drop in pressure followed by another rush of spumey wind, and a heavy wave of seawater washed through, sweeping Bonnet off his feet. He grabbed onto fissures in the chalk wall, clinging there like a crab with his one free hand, watching as the Baron was swept back toward the stairs as he fought to steady himself while keeping the pistol dry. The Gladstone bag whirled away and hid itself in the darkness. Bonnet stood up, the hammer held high, and rushed forward before the Baron righted himself and took aim. He flailed away with the hammer, catching him on the shoulder and neck, the Baron attempting to fend him off with the hand that held the pistol. Bonnet hit the Baron's wrist with the flat of the hammer, and the pistol fell into the gruel of seawater and sand and buried itself.

Taking a two-handed grip on the hammer, Bonnet struck the Baron atop the head with all his force in order to end the horror, and the Baron collapsed face downward and lay still. Bonnet threw the hammer into the darkness, before reeling away to lean against the cave wall, his shoes and trousers heavy with seawater. Still breathing heavily, he staggered back to the Baron's side. The Baron did not apparently breathe at all.

"Bashed neeps," Bonnet said aloud. He began to giggle, then sobbed aloud, and then turned aside and vomited. He crouched there, his mind a blizzard, only aware of the roaring noise surging up behind him in the moment before the wave struck him, knocking him down and washing him forward. He collided with the Baron's body and then with the bottom stair, kicking his feet to get a purchase on the mealy sand, frantically looking for the Gladstone bag. There it sat, jammed beneath the bottom stair not six inches from his face. It was still upright, but the next wave would surely swamp it.

He leaned in behind the stair treads and fished out the bag. Hurrying now, he slogged to where he had hidden the books and retrieved them both. Up the stairs he went, hugging his treasures to him. He thrust himself back-first through the door, pausing for a moment to look back. The ocean blasted into the cavern, lifting the Baron's body half way to the chalk ceiling, spinning it around and carrying it down the passage into the darkness. Bonnet kicked the trap closed, and pinned it with the wooden bar.

Misty sunlight shone through the windows, which seemed wrong to him after all the darkness, and he knew he was half out

of his wits when he went out through the kitchen, swabbing the floorboards with his shoe soles so that he would leave no clear imprints. Outside he shivered in the thin fog, looking wildly around lest someone had returned to *Seaward*, but his only audience was a troop of gulls milling on the beach.

He thrust the book boxes into the Gladstone bag and clasped it shut, then loped around the corner of the house, down along the rear wall and around into the sheltered area between the house and the barrier wall. His wagon stood as he had left it, the ponies side by side. He sprang onto the seat, turned the wagon around, and fled away up the hill, only now thinking of what he would do next. He would be tolerably cold when night fell if he did not find a sheltered spot where he could change out of his wet clothing and build a fire. He drove the wagon into the woods and hid it behind the coppiced hedge, invisible from the ocean and the Cliff Road.

He sat for a moment, collecting himself, and then unclasped the bag, shoving the books aside to view the banknotes beneath—ten-pound notes, crisp and new and dry, in small stacks bound with ribbon.

"Hah!" he shouted aloud, but then his momentary happiness deflated like a pierced balloon when he realized that the Baron would scarcely have brought the money if murder and robbery had been intention. The Baron was an innocent man, and Bonnet had lost his mind and struck him down without a thought…

But of *course* he'd brought the money, knowing that Bonnet would want to be sure of it before revealing the books' hiding

place. And the Baron had been very quick with his pistol—unnecessarily quick. There was guilt to go around, Bonnet told himself. He glanced down now and saw the small bulge within his coat pocket. He fished out the damp, fifty-odd pounds that Alice had given him—Alice who had trusted him, sensing that he needed the money desperately, which he had, as God was his witness. This thought horrified him anew: God and Alice as witnesses to his duplicity and weakness and greed!

He began to weep, wondering now why he felt no remorse for killing the Baron. He *feared* the Baron, that was why, and he hated what he feared. Perhaps all men hated what they feared: it stood to reason that they did. But had he killed the Baron out of mere hatred?

"*I deny it,*" he shouted. The Baron had threatened to sell him to the Gobblin' Society, and would have, too. The Baron was inhuman. He had no moral conscience. He felt no guilt. He took what he wanted, and committed horrible crimes, and now Bonnet had served him out in the way the Baron had done to others, in the way that he deserved. And in any event the Baron was dead. "*So be it,*" he said aloud, and he thumped the palm of his hand on his knee.

At the top of the hill he turned down the Cliff Road in the direction of Broadstairs, thinking to bivouac in the woods where he wouldn't be seen. And even if he *was* seen, no one could know that he was guilty of a crime. No one would come for him. The Baron would not have confided in anyone. Tomorrow he would take the road south to Dover, keeping to byways, through Sutton Downs, perhaps, along his regular route.

THE GOBBLIN' SOCIETY

But *must* he take ship in Dover? *Must* he leave his native land? Bound for where? What of his ponies? His caravan? His books? Why not north instead?—to Clacton-on-Sea or Scarborough? He had left no evidence behind, after all—nothing that the police could lay at his feet, even if they found the body. And surely Southerleigh had better things to do with his time than to search all England merely to supply the Gobblin' Society with a broiled bookseller.

He opened the hatch behind the seat and set the Gladstone bag into the safety of the interior, remembering now the letter that Southerleigh had compelled him to write, the letter meant to draw St. Ives to his doom this very afternoon—a regret that would haunt Bonnet all the days of his miserable life. *Surely* St. Ives would have noted the histrionic tone and been suspicious, he told himself. *Surely* he would not have walked into a trap!

Southerleigh would almost certainly take St. Ives to Gobblin' Manor, not to eat him but to mesmerize him and send him elsewhere to be eaten...

Bonnet could scarcely breathe and his heart was beating high. He forced himself not to think of Alice, but could think of nothing else. He climbed down onto the ground, his mind alive with the idea of throwing himself from the top of the cliff.

"The rest is silence," he said aloud, but even to him the words sounded self-serving. Was suicide an act of will, he wondered, or the absence of that quality? It mattered little; he hadn't the courage to murder himself. He had tried once before and failed. The truth was evident: every road but one led to damnation.

....

CHAPTER Nineteen

ALONG THE CLIFF ROAD

A lice sat in the wagon within a shroud of fog, parked in front of Clayton's Furnishings at the edge of Northdown Road in the neighborhood of Cliftonville. She felt as if she'd been away from Broadstairs for a week. Two easy-chairs appeared in the open doorway on a wheeled cart, hauled by a stunningly slow boy named Gilly who had been inside fetching them out for the past fifteen minutes. They were too broad to pass through, and Gilly removed one, turned the other around, and squeezed through, depositing the one chair on the pavement and then going back in for the other. Two small wooden tables, a whimsical coat-rack with gargoyle hooks, and two footstools with tapestry tops and bun feet were safely aboard the wagon, the lot of it sitting on a dry tarpaulin, half of which hung down on the street side, ready to make a package out of the wagon's contents in order to keep the thick weather from soaking the tapestry and stuffing.

Not for the first time Alice wished that Finn was with her to help with the loading, but he was no doubt in Pegwell

by now, ferreting out toads. As soon as this thought formed in her mind, however, an omnibus came clattering along the rails in the center of the road, appearing out of the fog. It lurched to a stop, and Finn himself leapt out of it followed by Tubby Frobisher, who appeared to be excessively damp, a bloody kerchief tied around his head, his bowler pulled down over it. The horses stepped along again, the omnibus lurching away.

Finn leapt up onto a wheel spoke and said, "It's the Professor. They've taken him—the smugglers have—a half hour past. He's aboard their boat, moving down the coast, or so we believe."

"Gilly!" she shouted at the boy, who was coming out with the second chair. "Cease and desist! We must unload the wagon now!" The boy stared at her, blinking with doubt and confusion. "There's not a moment to lose, Gilly," she said, climbing down herself to take him in hand. Getting a closer look at Tubby, she said, "You're hurt."

"Nothing notable, Alice, but we must be off. Take the chair back inside, boy," he said to Gilly. "On the double, and then return with the cart."

Alice hurried into the shop herself, thinking of cousin Collier's secret society—his abject fear of them and of the haunted house, his wild warnings, none of which sounded in the least theatrical to her now. She pressed her palms against the fabric of her shoulder bag, feeling the hard outline of Collier's pistol, and then thought of Eddie and Cleo, whom she had left behind, thank God. "I must be away immediately," she said to Polly, the woman who stood at the counter. "Will you deliver my purchases to *Seaward* tomorrow morning?"

"Yes, ma'am, I'll see to it," Polly said to Alice, who was already moving toward the door. The wagon stood empty, the pieces unloaded onto the pavement, and Finn was sliding the removable wall of the wagon into its slots. Tubby climbed aboard and sat on the tarpaulin, which he settled around his shoulders. Alice drove, Finn seated beside her, the wagon swaying along at a good clip in no time, bound for the North Foreland Road and the Cliff Road beyond.

She told her companions the gist of Collier Bonnet's story, leaving nothing out—neither the gun he had given to her nor his fear of the wicked men who congregated in the old mansion on the hill above Dickens Cove. Tubby told her of the man Paddington—his referring to that very house, alleged to be an eating club—and of the wild-eyed note they had received from Bonnet, luring them to the harbour where they were betrayed, the crime apparently taking shape even as Alice and Bonnet were conversing in the Crown Tavern.

She fell silent, struggling to make sense of it. Could it be that Cousin Bonnet had turned into a behemoth of duplicity over the years? Even now it seemed to her that he had been too affected by his own tale for it to be entirely false. The only explanation was that he was under a sentence of death if he failed—a mere puppet of this secret society. "He gave me this," she said, passing Bonnet's note to Finn, who read it aloud for Tubby's benefit: "If worst comes to worst, remember the haunted house, but do not go alone."

"What on earth can he mean, Alice?" Tubby asked. "What sort of 'worst' is he referring to?"

"I haven't any earthly idea," she said, "but we're bound to find out. I believe that the steamship will bring Langdon to the old house before bearing away for France. I pray that they do, although it's a miserable prayer."

They were well along the Cliff Road now, sweeping past the turning to Lazarus Bay and bound for Dickens Cove. Soon she slowed the horses to a walk. For the next few moments the curve of the road would hide them from anyone coming up from the cove or down from the house on the hill, but very soon they and their wagon would be visible, perhaps being seen by their enemies and losing any chance of surprise.

Finn pointed ahead to a stand of trees with a weedy path alongside, and Alice turned from the road, the wagon bumping over grass and sticks until they were well hidden behind the foliage. They tied the horse to a sapling and walked along through the trees in single file, Tubby carrying his cudgel, Alice with her hand in her bag, gripping the pistol, Finn's big clasp knife at the ready in his hand. Alice considered telling him to put it away, but knew he wouldn't listen to her.

Very shortly they came to the lane that bore away upward on the one hand and on the other down to the cove. There was no one to be seen. The veiled sun was half sunk in the sea, and the only sounds were the breaking waves and the calling of gulls. Finn strode toward the edge of the cliff to look out over the ocean. Tubby set out to follow him, but immediately spotted the handkerchief fluttering from the signpost, and even from a distance recognized the crest.

CHAPTER Twenty

GILBERT COMES TO HIS SENSES

ilbert awakened in his chair, fuddled and wrinkled and with the vague memory of having eaten his weight in sweetbreads. Paddington had disappeared, as had the amontillado—two bottles, God help him—and the butler's tray also. Hearing voices, he sat up in his chair and tugged at his clothing, then reached for his handkerchief to wipe the drool from his cheek. He remembered abruptly that he had left it fluttering from the signpost, and was compelled to use the back of his hand instead.

"Mr. Gilbert Frobisher, I believe," someone unseen said to him.

Gilbert hoisted himself to his feet, realizing that he was still two-thirds drunk, and turned toward the voice, which emanated from a tall thin man wearing a pince-nez who smiled at him from a face full of ghastly teeth. "Indeed," Gilbert said. It occurred to him that his stomach was

threatening to disgorge itself, and he took measured breaths to steady it.

"My name is Southerleigh," the man told him. "Mayhew Southerleigh. I'm told you sampled the sweetbreads."

"You have not been deceived, sir. I sampled them by the pound, I'm afraid. Veal, I believe, although Mr. Paddington referred to them as beef. They struck me as too tender and unctuous to be beef." He leaned on his cane, happy to have the support, for his head was swimming. The very thought of the sweetbreads was appalling to him, but he was determined to do the friendly thing.

"You are apparently a gourmand, sir," Southerleigh said to him, "a gobbler, ha ha!" His accent sounded vaguely French, although comically so—fraudulent? He leaned forward and drew back his lips, exposing sharpened incisors and looking keenly into Gilbert's face. "Would you be...*surprised* to discover that the meat was slightly more...exotic?"

"Game, perhaps?"

"Of a sort."

Paddington and Larsen entered now, both of them in high spirits. It seemed to Gilbert that the atmosphere of the room had altered in some way that could not be explained merely by the coming of evening. Perhaps it was his uneasy digestion. The newcomers took their places by the fire, smiling broadly at Gilbert with something close to menace, and it came to him with a dead certainty that he had been a fool. He glanced at the door, which was too far away. They would be on him before he took two strides.

"Have you ever eaten...*human* flesh, Mr. Frobisher?" Southerleigh whispered.

"Decidedly not," Gilbert told him.

"Are you quite certain?"

Gilbert was struck with anger, his sense of humor buried by a vicious headache. "Do I have the appearance of a damned cannibal?" he asked.

Southerleigh snorted with laughter. "I'm not a believer in damnation, so I cannot answer in the affirmative. As for your having the appearance of a cannibal, you have only to look into a mirror to see one."

"I see that I'm being practiced upon," Gilbert said. "I'm sorry to say that I've taken ill—the wine, perhaps. I'm scarcely in the mood for humor."

"This *is* uncommonly droll, to be certain, but there's no foolery in it. You've willingly consumed both the human pancreas and thymus glands in prodigious quantity and, according to your own testimony, quite happily. I congratulate you, sir. In so doing you have nominally joined the ranks of the Gobblin' Society, and the lot of us are in favor of your being a member in full."

Gilbert was seized with nausea, and he turned quickly toward the only open receptacle in the room—an elephant's foot umbrella stand adjacent to the door. He stooped over it and emptied the contents of his stomach in a long bout, which left him weak. His head swam, but he understood quite clearly what he had been told, and something within him knew that it was true. He bent over the elephant's foot again as if afraid of

another bout, and as he began hacking and spitting, he glanced at the door-handle, within arms reach now.

But his thought was cut short by a firm grip upon his arm, and someone—Paddington—blocked the door just behind him. He was clearly a prisoner. He still held his walking stick, but striking someone would not answer unless they tried to take his stick from him. This was a den of villains, and no doubt about it. He realized that it was Southerleigh who had hold of his arm, and the man patted Gilbert on the back solicitously. "Emptied out, are you?"

"Quite," Gilbert said. He wished to God that Tubby were with him. The two of them would clear the decks, and no mistake. But alone… "Help me to my chair, Mr. Southerleigh, if you will. I'm afraid that I was momentarily indisposed. It was not a comment on the quality of the food, whatever its source."

"Here's a wipe," Southerleigh said, handing him a napkin.

As Gilbert was patting his mouth a muscular servant entered the room, picked up the elephant's foot, and went out again. "I'll admit that I have in fact tasted human flesh while visiting an island in the South China Sea, Pangolina by name," Gilbert told them. It was a lie, but it would perhaps placate them. "Would you like to hear the tale in full?"

"We would like nothing better," Southerleigh said.

"Well, sir, we were feasted by the King of the island, which was a cannibal island, or had that repute, and skewers of meat were passing round. I was given a human hand, baked in the ground, I was told, and it would have insulted the King not to partake of it, for it was considered a delicacy. I adhere to the

old saying: 'When you go to Rome, do as Rome does.'" Gilbert smiled at his companions, hoping the lie had gone home.

"Very apt," Southleigh said to him. "What did you think of it? Did it eat well?"

"Tolerably so, yes, particularly the cracklings. It was not hearty fair, by any means, but perfect to whet the appetite."

"By golly we'll put it onto the menu," Southerleigh said. "You've found yourself among fellow travelers, sir. We would be quite happy if you would consider our offer. We're an eccentric band to be sure, but I can assure you that we profit by our eccentricities. Now, I'll be candid: there is a fee to join our little club, along with yearly dues, as is the case in any club in the land, but all of us have profited many times over by being members. It's an elite society."

"I'll consider it," Gilbert said. "Indeed I will. You've surprised me with the nature of your offer, however. I owe my success to… to the art of *consideration*."

"As do we all," Southerleigh assured him.

"Would you like to meet my cousin Hobbes?" Paddington asked. "They're bringing the gig around within a quarter of an hour to take him to the station, and it was he who brought us together, so to speak."

"I would like nothing better," Gilbert said. He was steadier now, and he pushed himself to his feet, both hands on the ball at the top of his stick.

"He resides in the taproom upstairs, taking a pint of porter before he embarks on his journey. Porter is a restful beverage to be sure—a natural sedative."

Gilbert found himself on the stairs, closely preceded and followed. At the top of the flight was a broad landing, with hallways stretching away on either side. They entered a room hung with grisly paintings of dismembered body parts and with a long table in the center. The door banged shut behind them, and Southerleigh strode across to yet another door.

A wave of cold air washed out of the room, which grew colder as Gilbert approached, the place reeking of ammonia like an ice-house. The reek enlivened Gilbert's brain, waking him fully, and when he entered he saw that this was no taproom. Cold storage was more like it. There were heavily curtained windows in the outside wall and sconces hissing here and there, the floor beneath them black with coal dust. A wooden armchair sat in the middle of the room, and on one wall was a broad wooden panel hanging from wheels set on the channel in an iron railing. Along another wall stood a bloodstained butcher's table some eight feet long.

Southerleigh strode to the wooden panel, bowed deeply in Gilbert's direction, and slid the panel along on its wheels, opening a shallow closet where a dead man dangled upside down on the wall, his roped-together feet hanging from a metal hook. He had no head, and his midsection had been sliced open and cleaned out, his pancreas and thymus along with it, no doubt. The bone in his right thigh was exposed, the flesh having been cut away. Beneath him sat a long, metal trough piled with ice blocks, straw scattered over all.

"Hello, Julian!" Paddington shouted at the dead man. "Here is Gilbert Frobisher, come to make your acquaintance!" He

laughed like a madman, and Larsen joined in. Gilbert felt faint again, and he staggered to the armchair where he sat down hard. He found that he was shivering with cold now, and the reek of ammonia made his eyes water.

The ape-like servant looked in just then and said, "The ship is in the offing, sir, and the boat has put off with our man aboard. I saw the coffin across the thwarts."

"Unlock the front gate and open it, Jensen," Southerleigh told him. And then to Gilbert he said, "Here's a friend of yours come to dine with us, Mr. Frobisher—one more Roman to the feast, if you will. You have half an hour to the minute to practice the art of consideration, keeping in mind the old saying about the relative merits of the live dog and the dead lion, eh?" He gestured at the butchered corpse of Julian Hobbes by way of illustration.

"We have a motto of our own, my good sir, come down to us from ancient Rome: *Aut manduces aut manduceris:* Eat or be eaten."

CHAPTER Twenty-One

THE FIGHT AT DICKENS COVE

"It is clear that Uncle ventured alone from the hotel to look in on this eating society that the man Paddington told us about," Tubby said, yanking Gilbert's handkerchief from under its sliver of wood. "He left his wipe, knowing that if it fell out badly we might come looking. He wasn't far wrong. I won't say that he did it to spite me, but…"

"God help him," Alice said. "Collier was terrified by the men who own this house."

"We'll do some terrifying of our own, by God. If…"

Tubby was interrupted by Finn's hasty return. "They're offshore," he said. "The steamship, and they've lowered a boat—six men rowing with a wooden box aboard, like those in the sea cave."

"If you give me the loan of your pistol, Alice, I'll murder the lot of them," Tubby said. "Your conscience can remain innocent. Mine has ceased to give a damn."

"My conscience has been dismissed from duty until we have Langdon and Gilbert returned to us," Alice said. "Then I'll reinstate it. And if Collier's fears are to be believed, we need to worry about ourselves into the bargain. As for the pistol, I fear that they'll hear any shooting from up the hill and might murder Gilbert out of hand."

"They'll *see* us, too, if we don't look sharp," Finn said, nodding in the direction of the road. "They'll be looking out for the steamer." Away above shone the lights of the old house. The mists had thinned, at least for the moment, and the moon was on the rise.

"Without the pistol, what chance have we against six men?" Tubby asked.

"There's big rocks in plenty there along the cliff," Finn said. "We'll be hid by the chalk and can pelt them as they come up where the way is narrow. The Professor will be safe in his box."

"Yes," Alice said, seeing no useful alternative. They moved down toward the cliff now, which was naturally crenellated with stone outcroppings and cut with channels that fell away toward the beach. The main trail led upward through a narrow defile, where the rocks would do their damage. The defile was visible from above for only a short distance, however: they'd have to make every stone do its work, or the men would run out of sight to the road, double back, and attack them before they could escape into the wood or any place else.

Alice looked about for other routes downward—escape routes. She saw that a person might creep down one particularly large fissure in the chalk, where there had been rockslides over

the years. It would be mortal, however, if someone pitched a rock from above—like clubbing fish in a chute, just as she and her two companions were about to do to a group of men she didn't know, men who could have little idea whom they were delivering to the old house. Thinking too much could paralyze a person, she thought, and turned away.

Tubby and Finn had set to work hauling head-sized rocks, bending along in order to keep from being seen by the men in the boat, who were remarkably close to shore now. Alice joined them, and very soon they had several piles, more than they'd have time to throw. She watched the boat come in through the surf now, a wave catching and lifting it, the boat rushing up onto the beach.

She glanced back at the house and couldn't see it from their vantage point, which was good, and the men on the beach would almost surely also be invisible until they appeared at the upper end of the defile. Four of them picked the box up by the handles at the corners, and, following the other two, they moved into the defile, six men in all, close together, trudging along without haste. She could hear the scraping of feet on the packed sand and gravel, the men muttering to each other. One laughed. They seemed to be taking an unconscionable amount of time and she had the abrupt urge to shout at them to hurry along, but just then they hove into sight, some forty feet below.

"Wait," Tubby whispered, poised with his rock over his head. "Now!" he said, and heaved his rock hard, striking the foremost man on the forehead and knocking him backward so that he bowled over the man behind him.

The injured man stayed down, at least for the moment, and the others looked around wildly. Alice and Finn hurled rocks now, which smashed against heads and shoulders and banged off the lid of the coffin, breaking a hole in it. The coffin bearers dropped the coffin, two of them falling under the hail of rocks, the two farthest back clambering over the coffin and the bodies of the men who blocked the sandy trail: two men down, and St. Ives struggling to tear open the broken coffin lid.

Tubby and Finn sprinted toward the road, Tubby with the pistol outstretched in his hand, and Finn with his clasp knife open, running like death-or-glory. Alice hurried to the fissure in the cliff, doubling the strap of her bag around her neck so that it hung down her back, and making her way downward as quickly as she could, clinging to the wet chalk wall and happy that she'd worn laced boots. She reached the bottom and set out running to the trail, heading upward now on firmer ground and expecting the sound of gunfire from above. She spotted the dropped coffin in the near distance, and she could see Langdon's hands working furiously to break the top open entirely.

"I'm here!" she shouted—the first words that came into her mind—and she gripped a bit fragment of wood, heaved it upward, and tore it free of the coffin, nearly falling over backward. She tore at another, Langdon's palm knocking it loose, and within moments he heaved himself free, rolling out onto the path and staggering to his feet. Alice embraced him, and they clung together for a long moment, hearts beating, until Alice said, "They're fighting on the road."

Langdon nodded, and both picked up long pieces of coffin lid before heading upward through the now-thickening fog. They stepped over two men, either dead or unconscious, and passed a third, who was dragging himself downward toward the cove and relative safety. By unspoken agreement they left him to his task, and within moments they came out onto level ground. The lights of the house on the hill were visible only as vague yellow rectangles, the fog having thickened. Tubby stood next to the signpost, leveling his pistol at three smugglers on the road, one of whom held a pistol of his own, aimed at Tubby. Finn stood behind Tubby, shielded by his body.

Alice's stick seemed pitiful to her. She carried her bag around her shoulder now, but it was even more useless, although there were pieces of chalk lying about that would turn it into a real head-knocker. She dared not move, however. It would simply call attention to herself and Langdon.

The three men were looking at Tubby, or more likely at Tubby's pistol, and neither Finn nor Tubby glanced in Alice's direction. Langdon gestured at her: almost certainly he meant to rush upon the man with the pistol and take him from behind. She shook her head: he was too far away—too much time for the man to turn around and begin shooting when they heard him coming...

Alice heard the sound of what must be a fairly heavy wagon coming along the road through the fog senselessly fast—a rattling and jingling and the pounding of hooves. The men on the road apparently saw the shadow rushing at them, but before they could move, a sort of Gipsy caravan burst into view, drawn by

two horses running hell for leather, the lunatic driver perched forward on his seat, his face a mask of wild determination. It was Collier Bonnet's perambulating library, driven by the man himself, chasing down redemption.

Langdon hauled the astonished Alice from the road. She saw Bonnet flicked his whip near the ear of the inside horse, which shied toward the smugglers, who were hunching away now, but too late. The horses and wagon bore two of them down and trampled them, the fore and aft wheels bouncing over their bodies as the wagon careened forward and out of sight around the bend in the road. Tubby shot the third man dead as he turned and sprinted toward the path to the cove. He sprawled in the weeds, still holding his pistol, and then Tubby turned to the struggling men lying in the dirt of the roadbed and said, "Lie still or I'll finish you."

Bonnet's caravan returned at a reasonable pace. Bonnet nodded at them as if there should have been no surprise at all in his sudden appearance, and leaped down from his seat. There was a dark look on his face, and he nodded his head sharply. As if he'd been rehearsing his part for weeks, he said, "Now let's see to the scoundrels in the house on the hill."

CHAPTER Twenty-Two

GOBBLIN' MANOR

H aving pushed back the window curtains, Gilbert stood looking down onto the carriage drive and the iron fence, his eyes searching the misty gloom for something that might change his luck for the better. He had heard the report of a pistol, but nothing had come of it. The sound had been fairly distant, however, and might have been masked by the carousing in the house: Gilbert might have been the only auditory witness. Southerleigh had mentioned that one of Gilbert's friends was coming to dine. He hoped to God that this was that friend, whomever he might be, and that he had come armed.

Minutes passed and still no one had come out of the house to investigate. There was no hullabaloo. All was as it had been within and without. Gilbert tried the window latch, which turned in its catch easily enough, but then he discovered that the window itself was fixed tight with heavy brass screws. And even if he could remove the screws, he

would have to grow wings to escape. Outside the window there was a small ledge and the limb of a nearby tree, but the ledge was narrow, and the limb would scarcely hold his weight.

He heard something from beyond the window now, out in the night. It sounded like people coming up the drive, making no effort to be quiet. They appeared out of the fog, four men carrying a coffin-sized box, lidless, a man lying within—St. Ives, by God! Gilbert thought of the smugglers' catalogue, the professor's name on the list. Was the Professor the man whom Southerleigh had named as the friend who would come to dine? The word "dine" took on a grim meaning…

But the big man in front…surely that was Tubby. Gilbert gasped in a great breath and clutched his forehead. *Certainly* it was Tubby, wearing a round hat and a coat that fit him like a sausage casing. He recognized Finn Conrad's jacket on the man beside Tubby. The other two were strangers to him, but certainly friendly strangers. He wished to heaven they knew he stood within this room, keeping company with a dead man.

His friends had come to rescue him, no doubt about it, but did they know what den of snakes they were walking into? As soon as the fiend Southerleigh recognized that they were frauds, all of Gilbert's playacting—the cannibal king and the roasted hand—would go straight out the window, and they would slit his throat.

Energized by this thought, he pushed the armchair across the floor and shoved it up under the latch on the door. He steeled himself and strode to the closet in the wall where, with a furious heave, he lifted Hobbes's body from its hook. He dragged it to

the window, plucked it from the floor by the rope that trussed the hands and legs, and with all his might pitched him through with a crashing great explosion of glass shards and broken mullions. Those on the path stopped and looked up, the corpse of Julian Hobbes slamming down not ten feet from them like an act of God.

LYING IN THE LIDLESS coffin and looking up at the grey mist through the trees, St. Ives considered what Bonnet had told them in the past few minutes—the cannibalism, the selling of mesmerized bodies to cannibal societies on the Continent, the soulless torture of innocent people who were lured into the society of monsters and were victimized.

He looked up into Alice's face, happy that she'd found him but wishing she were safely back at the Albion Hotel. A watch cap pulled down just above her eyes hid her hair and obscured her features. She had borrowed a pair of Bonnet's trousers along with the cap. The lighted portico was drawing near, and St. Ives prepared himself to spring out of the box.

There sounded a crashing noise from somewhere above, and he saw that the second story window had been smashed out of its frame. An apparently headless, naked corpse plummeted to the ground like a sack of sand. Gilbert Frobisher leaned out through the broken window and waved down at them before ducking back into the room.

They went on again, up the portico stairs, playing their roles. Their enemies could have no notion that six men had

come ashore in the boat, nor that three of them were dead and the other three tied up with two-inch line and gagged with kerchiefs. St. Ives closed his eyes now for effect. His wrists and ankles appeared to be bound, but the ends of the knotted rope were merely tucked in around him.

As his companions hauled him up the stairs onto the broad portico, he heard the door open and a voice—Paddington's voice—say, "Bring him inside and down the stairs into the chalk closet. Hurry. We've got a man causing a ruckus upstairs in the cold room. You four will subdue him post haste. We do not want to call attention to ourselves, tonight of all nights."

They were in through the door now, and the coffin was lowered to the floor. The moment it was settled, St. Ives leapt out, pushed the utterly surprised Paddington backward into a chair, and hit him hard with his fist. Paddington screamed and rolled off the chair onto the floor, scuttling away on his hands and knees, raising a hue and cry. There was a general shouting now, voices calling throughout the house. Watley the false constable and a man in a chef's jacket and toque rushed in, the latter carrying a heavy cleaver. The chef rushed at St. Ives, who snatched up a fireplace poker and parried his desperate stroke. Finn Conrad tackled the chef and bore him down, the man's head banging on stones of the hearth.

Watley hit Collier Bonnet over the head with a heavy brass candlestick and then bent over to strike him again when he fell. "No, sir!" Alice shouted at him, and swung her rock-heavy bag, knocking him to the floor, a blow so forceful that St. Ives, glimpsing it as he turned, was astonished at Alice's ferocity.

Finn leapt away as the chef swung the cleaver at his legs, missing him by a fraction of an inch. The man sprang to his feet, blocking St. Ives's crow-bar with his forearm and grasping his wrist. Tubby stepped up behind him and hammered him on the elbow with his cudgel when the man threw his arm back for another blow, the cleaver flying away and shattering the replica ship on the mantelshelf. The chef cringed away, begging Tubby for mercy, protesting his innocence, but at that moment the hulking brute who had driven the Baron's wagon rushed in carrying a heavy sword with both hands, and the chef fled back into the recesses of the house at a dead run.

"He's mine!" shouted Bonnet, and out from under his coat he drew a long revolver and shot the man calmly through the forehead, stepping forward and shooting him again, and then kicking him uselessly half a dozen times after he had collapsed in a heap, the blood running out of him.

In the silence that followed, St. Ives glimpsed a man fleeting past beyond the far door. It was Plank, the Harbour Master, carrying a painted wooden box. He was wearing a coat and hat, as if taking his leave. St. Ives ran after him, hearing Bonnet shout, "Take that book!"—an admonition that meant nothing to St. Ives. He followed the man at a distance, down a long, carpeted corridor, meaning to take him alive. Plank was the chief cutthroat, and no doubt about it.

Plank opened a door at the end of the hallway and ducked through it. The door banged shut, and St. Ives grabbed the latch and shook the door on its hinges, attempting to break it open. There was a sudden explosion from within the room, and a bullet

ripped through the door, blasting out big wooden splinters. St. Ives leapt back unhurt. Two more gunshots rang out in rapid succession, blowing a fist-sized hole through the door panel.

St. Ives heard the dim sound of running feet, and he reached in through the jagged hole, felt the latch until he found the locking mechanism, and opened the door. The lamp-lit floor was awash with papers and upended boxes, apparently flung around hurriedly, and the French window in the far wall stood open. St. Ives jumped through it and ran along a path into the wood, the trees towering around him through the fog.

The precariousness of his position came into his mind after he'd run fifty or sixty yards, however, and he stopped short, peering into the gloom and listening hard. Plank carried a pistol and was determined to use it. St. Ives again heard the sound of distant footfalls, although from which direction, he couldn't say. He set out once more, creeping along the weedy path, soon discovering that two other paths branched away from the first.

He studied the wet ground, but it was covered with flattened leaves and sticks, and there was no clear imprint, no reason to follow the right-hand track instead of the left. Either one might lead to a bullet in the head. He thought of Alice and the children and the future they would share if he simply gave up the chase and left Plank to the police. The Gobblin' Society was destroyed after all, or practically so.

He turned back, hurrying now, and saw a shadow coming toward him. The shadow resolved itself into Alice, who had shed her watch cap and loosed her hair, and who carried her rock-filled bag with the strap wrapped around her hand as if she

was ready to knock someone down. The sight of her made him want to weep, but there was no time to exchange avowals of love and gratitude, and they hurried together back to the mansion, where they found their enemies trussed up securely and Tubby and Finn standing on the lawn outside.

Gilbert Frobisher, holding on to his walking stick, stood precariously on a tree branch outside the broken window. "Did you leave any of the blighters for me?" he called down to them.

"Not a one!" Tubby shouted, and in that moment there was a loud cracking noise, and the branch snapped off and fell, taking Gilbert with it. He struck a second branch a few feet below, but that limb gave way almost at once, and he dropped the last few feet onto the headless corpse that had once been Julian Hobbes. Tubby helped his uncle to his feet, and Finn fetched the fallen walking stick.

"Fancy being saved from death by a dead man," Gilbert said, looking down at the body, and then, aware of his untimely levity, he apologized to Alice and advised her to avert her eyes.

Alice was already looking around her, however. "Where is cousin Collier?" she asked.

But no one could tell her. He had quite disappeared.

THE FINAL CHAPTER

Alice sat looking out at the beach in the very same room at *Seaward* that she had occupied for weeks on end as a girl. The big room hadn't changed a whit, and almost certainly had been closed up for the long years since. She and Langdon had forced open the door, which had been jammed against the uneven floorboards, and along with Finn's help they had spent the day turning out the furniture and cleaning the room from top to bottom, filling the iron log rack, beating the carpets, replacing the candles in the sconces, and topping up the oil in the lamps. The new furnishings had come down from Clayton's this morning, including a mattress and bed-clothes, the two stuffed chairs, and the other odds and ends hurriedly removed from their hired wagon just yesterday.

An hour ago the constable had appeared to collect the Baron Truelove's body, which had washed ashore some time in the night. Alice had discovered it while on an early

morning walk, thinking from a distance that it was a dead seal entangled in kelp and flotsam. What had appeared to be seal-skin had turned out to be the Baron's cloak. Crabs were making a meal of his flesh, scuttling over wounds on his head and foot and snapping off bits with their scissor-like pincers. He was a ghastly sight, staring sightlessly at the sky, his mouth agape, a crab busy picking at his swollen tongue.

She had thought of the beached whale that her uncle had intended to blow up with dynamite, and she wondered whether she would ever be entirely rid of the Baron, who was starting to stink now that the sun was up over the woods. She had fetched the old coracle out of the storage room and upended it over his body, where it had lain throughout the day, the surf running in and washing around it, but steadfastly refusing to take the body back.

THE CASEMENT WINDOWS STOOD open now, the sun declining, a small sea breeze blowing in and scouring out lingering shadows. Alice watched as Langdon and the constable appeared below, coming from the direction of the sea cave. The two of them had gone off to look into the cave some time past, something that Alice had no mind to do. The constable, carrying a cloth valise, climbed into his wagon now and rattled away, the Baron's body still covered by the coracle.

Alice left the window and arranged a decanter of sherry and a plate of shortbread biscuits on the table between the easy chairs. She sat in one of the chairs, settled her stockinged feet

onto a foot-stool, and thought of nothing at all until Langdon walked in and sat opposite her, looking like ruination with the livid bruise on the side of his forehead. She poured each of them a glass of sherry and offered him a biscuit.

"Will I tell you what we found in the sea cave?" Langdon asked after sampling the biscuit and sherry.

"Not more coffins and corpses, I hope."

"No. We found the baron's hat, oddly enough. It was exactly as you thought when you discovered his body. He almost certainly died in the cave and was drawn out into the ocean by the outgoing tide and cast ashore again."

"Why would the Baron have gone into the cave at all?" Alice asked. "The coffins were gone away. Surely he had no interest in limpets and barnacles."

"It's a complete mystery. Aside from his hat, we discovered the head of a hammer, the handle broken off short, and also a pistol with several empty chambers. The Baron's foot had been shot-through, as you know, and his head had most likely been bashed in with the hammer. There was a broken lantern also—two of them. He had met someone, do you see, and the meeting had turned deadly."

"Did you mention cousin Collier at all when you were chatting with the constable?"

"I did not."

Alice nodded and sipped her sherry, which was first rate, one of a dozen bottles that Gilbert had given her before he and Tubby had set out for Gilbert's home in Dicker at mid-day. They'd be well along the road by now.

"Are we bound by *morality* to mention cousin Collier? Perhaps as a matter of duty? I noted a laceration on his cheek last night and what appeared to be blood on his trousers. It might have been the Baron's blood."

"It might as easily have been his own—a shaving accident, say."

She thought for a moment about the nature of duty, duty to the law and duty to one's family, which might sometimes be contradictory, and then said, "A shaving accident would surely explain it. Occam's razor comes to mind."

"Indeed it does," he said, smiling at her. "And why embroil a possibly innocent man in this terrible business? To what end? Not justice, surely. The note with his signature on it has disappeared. The Gobblin' Society is forcibly disbanded, and the few men still alive who know of his activities would scarcely mention his name. They have much to lose and little to gain. And in any event, the lot of them will hang for the murder of Julian Hobbes."

"I won't weep for them," Alice said. The two fell silent until Alice said, "I'll admit that there's something self-serving in my attitude. I feel considerably lighter now that Collier has gone away and is safe from both the Gobblin' Society and the police. He seems to be quite happy lending his books for pennies and shillings to people in out of the way places, and he deserves some happiness."

Langdon had fallen asleep in his chair, however, and she watched him for a time, scarcely able to believe that the turmoil of the past twenty-four hours had been anything but a dream.

She poured more sherry into her glass and looked around the room in which they sat. It was a good room in a good house, houses being good or bad, light or dark, depending on who occupied them, depending on whether they loved the house or were indifferent to it. Marriages were much the same, it occurred to her. She thought about the years of their marriage, of the strange things they'd seen and done, and how the years passed away deliriously quickly.

And now, having done quite enough thinking, she arose and went to the bank of east-facing windows and watched the sun disappear into the sea. Then she set about shutting and latching the casements, the wind having grown chill with the setting sun.